"Why, Tanner? Why pursue me when you could have any woman in town?" Amanda asked.

"I don't want any woman. I want you." His arm snaked out and pulled her solidly against his chest. Tipping her head back, he bent so close their lips were almost touching. "Make no mistake, Amanda. This is not love. I stopped loving you a long time ago."

She could scarcely breathe. Something in her had never forgotten the wild, wanton love of Tanner Donovan. She fought the truth, but she couldn't shut it out of her mind. "What's this for, then? Lust? Revenge?"

"You've been a fever in my blood for years. The only way to get you out of my system is to bed you . . . one more time."

She put her hand on his chest and shoved. For all the effect she had, she might have been a snowflake battering a mountain.

"I take what I want, Amanda. And I want you."

It was not so much a kiss as an assault. His lips were hard on hers, demanding, expert. The kiss was passionate, persuasive, dangerous, and she could feel the fierce yearning and soft yielding of her body. Another moment with his lips on hers and she would be lost. . . .

WHAT ARE *LOVESWEPT* ROMANCES?

They are stories of true romance and touching emotion. We believe those two very important ingredients are constants in our highly sensual and very believable stories in the *LOVESWEPT* line. Our goal is to give you, the reader, stories of consistently high quality that may sometimes make you laugh, sometimes make you cry, but are always fresh and creative and contain many delightful surprises within their pages.

Most romance fans read an enormous number of books. Those they truly love, they keep. Others may be traded with friends and soon forgotten. We hope that each *LOVESWEPT* romance will be a treasure—a "keeper." We will always try to publish

LOVE STORIES YOU'LL NEVER FORGET
BY AUTHORS YOU'LL ALWAYS REMEMBER

The Editors

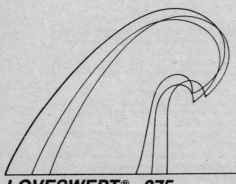

LOVESWEPT® • 275
Peggy Webb
Sleepless Nights

 BANTAM BOOKS
TORONTO • NEW YORK • LONDON • SYDNEY • AUCKLAND

SLEEPLESS NIGHTS
A Bantam Book / August 1988

*If you would be interested in receiving protective vinyl
covers for your Loveswept books, please write to this address
for information:*

Loveswept
Bantam Books
P.O. Box 985
Hicksville, NY 11802

ISBN 0-553-21876-X

Published simultaneously in the United States and Canada

PRINTED IN THE UNITED STATES OF AMERICA

O   0 9 8 7 6 5 4 3 2 1

*For Henry, who aided me in
the Great Scholarship Search;
And to his beautiful wife Martha,
who understood.*

One

"Tanner Donovan looks every bit as handsome as he did when he was quarterback at Greenville High. Maybe better."

Amanda Lassiter felt an odd breathlessness at the mention of his name. She must be crazy, she decided. Eleven years was time enough to forget anything, even a man as sinfully delicious as Tanner.

She made herself hang the antique petticoat carefully, before turning around to answer her assistant and longtime friend. "No doubt he'll set the hometown girls aflutter, Maxine. His wealth and fame are exceeded only by his reputation." She hoped her voice conveyed exactly the right blend of nonchalance and disinterest.

"You've kept up?"

"No. I've read the papers, like everybody else." Amanda sat down at her desk.

Maxine arched her eyebrows and tapped the newspaper with one long red fingernail. "How long has it been since you've seen him?"

"Not since the wedding."

Maxine didn't have to ask which wedding Amanda

meant. Folks had talked about it for five years afterward. Some of them were still talking. "I'll never forget the way Tanner Donovan looked when you walked down that aisle with his best friend."

Neither would Amanda, but she certainly didn't want to dredge up the past. "It's ancient history."

"Not as ancient as you might think. Just last week I overheard a group of young men at Doe's Restaurant talking about the way Tanner stormed down that aisle and lifted you in his arms when the preacher asked if anyone knew any reason why you and Claude shouldn't be joined in marriage. They even quoted exactly what he said, 'I know because she's still in love with me.' That story is legend around here. The local kids love it."

Amanda's knuckles turned white as she clutched the edge of her desk. Damn the man! She closed her eyes as the memory washed over her. Tanner, sweeping her into his arms, challenging her with fierce quicksilver eyes to deny his words; and Claude, standing loyally by, as he always had; Claude, representing stability and children and a home; Claude, loving her, always loving her. She'd loved him too—but it hadn't been enough. The memory of Tanner was always there between them. Looking back now, it amazed her that they'd stayed married for six years. She'd wondered a hundred times since that fateful day what her life would have been like if she'd kept quiet, if she'd let Tanner abduct her.

"You're bound to hear all sorts of things if you eavesdrop," she said now.

Maxine chuckled. "If I didn't eavesdrop, what would we talk about at bridge club? Besides, that's all I have to do since I'm temporarily between husbands." She looked down at the photograph of Tanner Donovan. "That man's enough to set the old motor revving. While he's home for the holidays I might take a crack at him myself. That is, if you don't have plans for him."

"I moved back to Greenville to open a business, not to try to renew an old romance. What happened between Tanner and me is over and done with." Her cool smile was very convincing. "You have my blessing. Not that you need it, of course."

"Maybe you'd better look at this before you dismiss him." She plopped the newspaper on Amanda's desk. "I'm already in overdrive from looking at his picture."

Amanda pushed the newspaper aside without glancing at it and smiled at her irrepressible friend. Maxine had breezed in and out of divorce court so often—four times at the last count—that the judge had declared his intentions of putting in a revolving door just for her. However, her apparent unsuitability for the bonds of matrimony didn't keep her from the hunt. She stalked men with lusty good cheer, and it appeared she'd chosen Tanner Donovan as her latest quarry. Amanda was surprised that the idea caused a little twinge of regret.

"Do you think you can gear down long enough to help me move this case of jewelry before we close up? With Christmas coming, people will be looking for gifts, and these antique brooches will be perfect."

For the next twenty minutes they worked together taking out the brooches, moving the small case closer to the front of the shop, and rearranging the jewelry. After the shop door swished shut behind Maxine, Amanda locked up and returned to her desk. Picking up the newspaper, she stared down at the front-page spread on Tanner Donovan. The man's dazzling charm, which she remembered so well, was not diminished by the black-and-white photograph.

Her eyes scanned the column. "Greenville's most famous native son, Tanner Donovan, businessman-philanthropist, will be on hand for Saturday night's American Diabetes Association charity benefit. Mr. Donovan, former outstanding quarterback for the Texas Titans, has contributed $100,000 to this worthwhile charity. His longtime interest in diabetes . . ." Amanda stopped reading and sat staring into space. Unconsciously she caressed the photograph.

"Where did we go wrong, Tanner?"

The sound of her own words startled her into action. Picking up her bag and her hat, she started for the back door. Her little blue Honda Civic was parked behind her shop. She tilted her hat at a cocky angle, climbed behind the wheel, and headed toward her favorite coffee shop on the river. She'd be damned if she was going to sit around wallowing in self-pity, guilt, and old memories.

From his first glance of the river, Tanner was glad he'd decided to drive from Dallas instead of taking his private jet. He pressed a button to lower his windows so he could sniff the air. Home. There was no place like it. Never slackening his speed, he took in everything—the rich, black land stretching out flat as far as the eye could see, sliced through and nourished by the muddy waters of the Mississippi; the massive oaks, drab with their brown winter leaves but no less magnificent; the whitewashed fences, dividing the Delta into neat, clean sections, signifying that man had conquered and tamed at least part of the land.

Tanner laughed aloud with the sheer delight of being alive. Being home always made him feel this way. No matter how many years he'd lived in Dallas, he still thought of Greenville as home.

He shot his car across the bridge, the red Corvette picking up speed as he whipped in and out of the Friday afternoon traffic with the ease that comes from practice. Just across the bridge he spotted the café, Jimmy's. His stomach turned over. Whether it was from hunger or memories, he didn't know. Nor did he bother to question it; he simply followed his instinct.

He glided the red Corvette smoothly off the road and brought it to a stop in the gravel parking lot in front of the one-room, clapboard café. Tanner removed his cashmere jacket the minute he stepped outside. It was hot—too hot for December, he thought.

As he tossed his jacket back onto the front seat of his car, he saw the woman. She had the kind of legs men dream about, and the kind of walk that could start revolutions. Tanner lounged against his car, enjoying one of his favorite pastimes, girl watching. Even from the back he could tell that she was beautiful. Anything less than perfection of face would be a sacrilege on that body. He let his eyes move up to her waist. It was tiny, nipped in by a wide leather belt. He stiffened as she took off her felt fedora and shook out her hair. In the late afternoon sun the tresses blazed with dazzling copper highlights. He remembered only one woman who had hair like that—Amanda Lassiter. As far as he knew, she was still living in Missouri. And he hoped to hell she stayed there.

He pocketed his keys and headed toward the café.

People stopped talking when Tanner walked through the door. He was big and handsome, and he exuded the kind of power generated by a storm rolling off the river. Standing inside the door, he let his gaze roam, taking in the silver plastic bells hanging over the cash register, the glass case of coconut cream pies, and the crowded wooden booths. She was at the back of the room, sitting beside the window that overlooked the river, her head bent over a menu. Amanda Lassiter.

For a moment he went a little crazy inside. He wanted to march across the room, jerk her into his arms, and throw her into the river. Hard on the heels of that thought came another even more disturbing one. He wanted to gather her close to him and kiss her until they were both breathless. He wanted to strip the clothes from her body and kiss every inch of that perfection—just as he had so many years ago.

Forcing himself to steady his breathing, he started across the room. She looked up and their gazes clashed. He saw her catch her breath. Her reaction pleased him. He didn't know why but it did. He saw her hands tighten on the menu, but she never looked away. Her glorious aqua eyes focused, sure and steady, on his as he walked to her booth.

He didn't stop until he was standing over her, so close that he could smell her scent. Jasmine. Sweet and sultry. Exactly the way he remembered.

"See anything you like?" he asked.

"Why? Are you selling something?"

She was still the same spirited Amanda. He was glad. "No, I'm giving it away."

"Pity. You could have been rich."

"I am." He slid into the opposite side of her booth. "Mind if I join you?"

"Would it make any difference if I said no?"

"No." He reached across the table and took her left hand. The cool touch of her slim ivory fingers almost made him forget what she'd done to him. "I see you've taken off the ring."

She lifted quizzical brows but said nothing.

"My parents keep me informed." He let her hand drop. "They seem to think I'm still interested in the doings of my two former best friends."

"Are you?"

He took a certain malicious pleasure in thinking that he was the cause of the breathless catch he heard in her voice.

"No. Simple idle curiosity." He hoped he'd lied with a straight face. He flipped open a menu. "Are you having the hot chocolate?"

"Yes, with marshmallows."

It was the first time she'd smiled since he'd walked through the door. Amber lights lit briefly in the center of her aqua eyes, then faded as quickly as they had come. It was the first time he'd seen that smile in eleven years.

Tender feelings tried to blossom in his soul, but he quickly squashed them.

"Claude never liked marshmallows. I would have thought you'd have picked up new habits living with him. Six years, wasn't it?"

Her tongue flicked over her lips before she answered. "Yes."

He remembered so well the feel of that tongue. "Don't do that," he wanted to shout. Instead he signaled to the waitress. "Two hot chocolates with marshmallows." Turning to Amanda, he asked, "Anything else?"

"Solitude."

"We don't always get what we want, Mandy, love." He was as startled as she was when the affectionate term slipped out. For a moment her expression grew soft; then that familiar cool mask of indifference slipped back across her face.

"I'm not interested in a trip down memory lane, Tanner."

"Neither am I. One time through hell is enough for me."

Her eyes sparkled with anger. "It was a hell of your own making."

"That's debatable. There's not much a man can do when he's in another state and his two best friends are playing footsie behind his back."

"How could you possibly have noticed? You never left the football field long enough."

They glared at each other until Tanner began to feel conspicuous. More than that, he felt the stirrings of emotions he wanted to remain buried. He forced himself to lean back and relax.

"Why don't we start over?"

"As you said, one time through hell is enough."

He felt a small glimmer of satisfaction in knowing that she'd been hurt too. "I'm not talking about the past. I'm talking about our conversation." Abruptly he stood up and took her hand. He felt it tremble as he placed a kiss in her palm. "Miss Amanda Lassiter, do you mind if I join you? I'm home for the holidays, and you're the first friend I've seen." He slid back into the booth.

"Am I?" Her voice reminded him of velvet—soft, smooth, and beautiful.

"Are you what?"

"Still your friend?"

He studied her lovely face in silence. That face had haunted his dreams, teased his imagination, fired his passion, and kindled his anger for the past eleven years. Were they still friends? No, he thought. Adversaries, yes. Former lovers, yes. But friends?

"I don't think so," he said quietly. "However, since we're both home for the holidays and probably will be running into each other, I see no reason to make it unpleasant."

"I'm not home for the holidays. I live here."

His parents hadn't told him that. "Since when?"

"Since April. I've opened an antique clothing shop on Washington Street."

"And Claude?"

"He's still in Fulton, Missouri, running the local newspaper. I never should have stayed there as long as I did. After the divorce it was awkward—for both of us."

He felt a sudden rush of compassion for Claude. It would have been more than awkward; it would have been torture. Losing Amanda after having possessed her was bad enough. He knew. For Claude, seeing her every day and not being able to touch her must have been sheer hell. At least Tanner hadn't had to go through that. After the wedding he'd gone straight to football camp and the blessed oblivion of a demanding career in professional sports.

His compassion for Claude quickly changed to a cold rage as he thought of the two of them together. It was an image he'd tried to block out over the years. With Amanda sitting across the table from him, the image took on a clarity that made him want to smash his fists into the wall. His gaze swept hungrily over her, and he decided the only way to block out that vision was to replace it. He imagined Amanda in his arms . . . sweet yielding flesh . . . drowning himself in her softness.

His loins tightened almost painfully, and he thought he must be going mad. The arrival of the hot chocolate saved his sanity.

They sipped for a while in silence, watching each other over the rims of their cups.

"Age has improved you, Tanner."

He grinned. "I like to think it's practice, not age."

"I wouldn't know about that, you wicked man. I

was talking about your looks. You're bigger, of course, more solid. But also more mellow."

"More broken."

"I read about your knee. I'm sorry."

"It cut short my career, but I can't complain. Maybe it was for the best. Some men stay in pro ball too long. Way past their prime." He watched her eyes darken as he reached across the table and cupped her chin. "And you, Amanda." His fingers caressed her jawline. "Don't pull away, I've been wanting to touch your skin since I walked into this café. Magnolia blossoms must wilt with envy when you walk by."

She laughed. "Still glib of tongue."

"I keep in practice." He released her and stuck his hand in his pocket so she wouldn't see it shaking. "Even at thirty-three, after all these years, you're still the most beautiful woman I've ever seen."

"Thank you, Tanner. At thirty-three, you're still the smoothest talking man I've ever met. No wonder I fell in love with you when I was eighteen."

"Seventeen. It was right before your birthday, remember?"

A peculiar stillness settled over her, but her eyes never wavered.

"I don't want to remember, Tanner."

Silently he applauded her spirit. "Neither do I." He finished the last of his chocolate and picked up the check. "My treat."

"I don't want anything from you."

Their gazes locked. Everything that had been between them seemed to sizzle in the air—the passion, the betrayal, the guilt, the hatred. Tanner was the first to break the spell. He knew that if he didn't walk away now, he never would.

"And I don't want anything from you, Amanda." He stood up swiftly, taking the check with him.

"Consider this payment on an old debt, an apology for trying to steal you from Claude at the altar."

"Done." She picked up her hat and set it on her head again at the same jaunty angle. "I suppose I could have demanded blood. You're getting off lightly."

"The next time I'll send diamonds. So long, Amanda." Giving her a smart salute, he turned toward the cash register.

"There won't be a next time."

He heard her but kept walking. He decided it was better to let her have the last word than to risk turning back. If he looked into those aqua eyes one minute longer, he'd have her in his arms right in the middle of Jimmy's, scandalizing half the population of the Delta.

He paid for the chocolate and got into his car without looking back. Grimly he turned the key in the ignition and set a hell-bent-for-leather course across town. Tanner Donovan was going home, and nothing was going to spoil his homecoming. Not even Amanda Lassiter.

Amanda sat at the booth long after he had gone. She felt as if her heart had just been ripped out and stomped on. Pressing her knees together under the table, she forced herself to sit still until she could calm down. Dear heaven, she'd had no idea that seeing Tanner again would affect her like this. It had been eleven years. Eleven years!

Curious faces began to turn in her direction. She met their stares with her head up. Damn Tanner Donovan. She wasn't going to let this encounter get the best of her. She had to live in this town. Pasting a bright smile on her face, she stood up and walked across the room. She even managed to put a smart spring into her step and to call out a few cheerful greetings.

Her car seemed a million miles away, but she was finally inside. While the engine was warming up, she turned and looked down the road. There was no sign of Tanner. Not even a lingering puff of dust marked his departure.

Putting her car into gear, she headed home. "Out of sight, out of mind," she said aloud, but even as she spoke, she knew she was lying.

Two

Amanda could hear the music all the way out in the parking lot—"White Christmas," played by Greenville's Jazz Combo with more enthusiasm and optimism than skill. Smiling, she locked her car and started toward the clubhouse alone. Her escort for the evening, Walter Cummings, had called the night before with fever, a hacking cough, and profuse apologies.

It was just as well, she decided. Since the previous day's encounter with Tanner Donovan, she'd been poor company for everybody. Her Friday night bridge party had been a disaster. She and Maxine had been set twice because of her crazy bidding. Once she'd bid four hearts with nothing in her hand except the queen and a jack—and all because she was thinking of the way Tanner Donovan's pants fit. She wondered if five years of deprivation had warped her mind. She wasn't going to dwell on it.

Holding her elegant head high, she pushed open the door and entered the Greenville Country Club.

Amanda's entrance caused a stir. It wasn't just her head-turning beauty, nor her dress—a twenties-style ivory satin gown that clung to her body like a lover. It was the anticipation. Greenville residents, who could remember the way Tanner Donovan had raged when Amanda Lassiter walked down the aisle with his best friend, wondered what would happen with the two of them in the same room all evening.

They weren't long in finding out.

Amanda had barely cleared the doorway when she saw him coming. She felt a melting warmth all the way down to her toes. In a tuxedo, Tanner could be declared illegal. Broad-shouldered, slim-hipped, solid, and well toned, he was unmistakably an athlete. A delectable one. As she watched him move, a bright memory flashed through her mind—Tanner lying beside her on the riverbank, sunlight gilding the dark hairs that shadowed his sweat-slickened chest, his blue jeans riding low on his narrow hips. Her throat constricted and her palms dampened, but she couldn't turn away. She had a strange premonition that this encounter had been arranged by fate.

Her head went up in a regal gesture, and she smiled.

"If that smile's designed to make me forget every other woman in this room, then you've succeeded." Tanner had stopped so close beside her that she could count the fine laugh lines fanning out from his eyes.

"I don't wear the smile by design. It's just my natural good humor."

She loved the way his eyes lit up when he laughed. He was laughing now.

"Did anybody ever tell you modesty is a virtue?" he asked.

"They did, but I never believed them."

"Neither did I."

His gaze raked over her boldly. She could feel

his eyes on her, like hands searching, touching, caressing. They lingered over her cleavage and, moving upward, hungrily studied her lips. Her body's response was instantaneous. As if it had been only yesterday since they'd loved, she felt her nipples tighten against the revealing satin of her gown.

He'd noticed. She could tell by the daredevil gleam in his eyes and the slight lifting of one cocky eyebrow.

"Am I disturbing you, Amanda?" he asked.

She wanted to shoot him.

"Don't flatter yourself."

"You disturb me." Reaching out, he gently lifted a strand of her copper hair and let it sift through his fingers. She stood still, afraid that any move she made would be straight into his arms. "As a matter of fact, you ruined a good night's sleep for me last night. I think you owe me for that."

"I thought we settled our debts yesterday."

"That was mine. This one is yours."

"I don't think they serve hot chocolate here. Will a glass of wine do?"

"I was thinking of something more substantial."

The hand that had been holding her hair dropped onto her shoulder and drifted down her back, tracing the deep vee of her dress all the way to her waist. She was determined that he not see how his touch affected her. She was the one who had left him; she was the one who had chosen a safe marriage with a good man instead of the frenzied competition with pro football for Tanner's affection; she was the one who had come between two best friends. She was also the one who had borne the burden of guilt. But she'd carried the load long enough. It was time to put Tanner Donovan behind her, once and for all.

"I'm substantial but not available."

He chuckled. "I think you are . . . and I intend to find out."

She looked directly into his eyes and smiled. "And I intend that you don't."

"So much the better. I love a good pursuit."

She laughed. "I don't plan to run. Running away is not my style."

"I remember your style, Mandy. I remember it so well."

The steam practically rose between them as their gazes clashed. She was the first to break the spell.

"Why, Tanner? Why pursue me when you could have any woman in town?"

"I don't want any woman in town. I want you."

"For old times' sake?"

"No." His arm snaked out and pulled her solidly against his chest. Tipping her head back with one finger, he bent so close that their lips were almost touching. "Make no mistake, Amanda. This is not love. I stopped loving you a long time ago."

"And I you." She could scarcely breathe or speak as realization slammed into her. A part of her still loved Tanner. The truth shook her to the core. She'd married Claude, had lived with him for six years, had *loved* him. But all the while something deep in her soul had never forgotten the wild, wanton love of Tanner Donovan. She fought against the truth, tried to shut it out of her mind, but how could she deny it when she was back in his arms and being there felt like heaven?

He would never know, she vowed. No one would ever know.

"Tell me, Tanner, if this pursuit is not motivated by love, what is the motivation? Lust? Revenge?"

"Catharsis." His arms tightened around her. "You've been a fever in my blood for eleven years. I've decided that the only way to purge you from my system is to bed you . . . one more time."

"Only once?"

He grinned. "You always were greedy."

"And you always were arrogant." She put her hand on his chest and shoved. For all the effect her attempt to push him away had, she might as well have been a snowflake battering a mountain.

"I take what I want. And I want you."

He took her mouth swiftly, greedily, without tenderness and without love. It was not so much a kiss as an assault. His lips were hard on hers, demanding, expert.

Not even for a second did Amanda consider struggling against him. His arms were like steel. Nor did she give a moment's thought to their audience. She and Tanner seemed fated to make public scenes. She did give thought to the kiss, however. It was passionate, persuasive, dangerous, and it threatened to topple her defenses. She could feel the rush of liquid warmth between her thighs, the fierce yearning and soft yielding of her body. Another moment with his lips on hers and she would be lost.

Her only defense would be to meet fire with fire. She slid her hands under his tuxedo jacket and began a slow, erotic circling on his back. The power behind the kiss shifted subtly as she boldly plunged her tongue into Tanner's mouth. His reaction was immediate. She felt, rather than heard, the moan deep in his throat, and then he was devouring her, feasting on her as if he would never let go.

They were caught in a time warp. They might have been high-school sweethearts again, young, idealistic, and very much in love—but they were not. They were two battle-scarred people, eleven years older and eleven years more cynical.

Tanner lifted his head and held her at arm's distance.

"I'd forgotten how well you kiss."

"That was just a sample. Something to lead you on."

"You make a fine quarry, Amanda. I'm going to enjoy the hunt."

"I'd be careful if I were you, Tanner. Sometimes the hunter ends up the hunted."

"And what are your intentions if you catch me?"

"Certainly not to bed you. But dishonorable nonetheless."

He grinned. "You always were an unpredictable woman. I can hardly wait."

"Don't hold your breath. I've provided all the fun I intend to for one evening."

"Does that mean you're turning down my offer of a warm bed and a willing body?"

"Precisely."

"Then I'll have to find a substitute." Releasing her, he gave a smart salute. "Have a good evening, Miss Lassiter."

"You, too, Mr. Donovan."

She stood there smiling, watching him walk away. Not by one twitch of an eyelash would she show that there was a cyclone raging inside her. She wouldn't run and she wouldn't flinch. She would stand firm against all his assaults, and she would win.

"What in the name of tarnation was that all about?"

Amanda turned to see Maxine standing at her elbow, her face shining with anticipation.

Maxine loved being the first one to hear a juicy story, but more than that she adored being the one to witness it. She had been standing near the punch table with a good view of everything that had happened between Tanner and Amanda, and she'd stepped on the feet of two people in her haste to be the first one to get to the source.

"You saw?"

"'Me and everybody else in Greenville. Good lord! I thought he was going to make love to you right here in the Country Club."

"That's his avowed intention, but I doubt that even he is bold enough to do it in public."

"Some women have all the luck." Then, remembering their conversation at the shop, she gave Amanda a quizzical look. "I thought you weren't planning to renew an old romance."

"I'm not. It's just a game we're playing."

"Some game! I'd love to be the winner. Shoot, I'd even love to be the loser." She sighed dramatically. "That man looks good enough to eat. He's a big old juicy steak, just waiting for some woman to bite in. Lord, he makes Wilford look like black-eyed peas."

Amanda laughed. "And where is the lucky Wilford Trentwell?"

"Hiding in the men's room, trying to get up enough courage to propose again."

"He proposed?"

"On the way over. I turned him down. Thought I might have a shot at Tanner Donovan, but it looks like I was wrong."

Amanda lost track of what Maxine was saying as she caught a glimpse of Tanner. He had wasted no time in finding another woman. He had Evelyn Jo Goff in a tight huddle on the dance floor. A blaze of jealousy coursed through her, and she wondered if he'd already found his substitute.

"Yes. I was definitely wrong." Maxine spoke loud enough to make Amanda jump.

"What?"

Maxine patted her frizzy blond hair, then reached over to pat Amanda's arm. "I said, 'Here comes Wilford.' And since I've already got him hooked and am probably going to say yes just because I can't stand this unholy state of unmatrimony, I'm going to be generous and let you have the first dance with him. Bring him back to me in one piece."

"Thanks. You're a real friend, Maxine."

"I know." When Wilford came within grabbing distance, she took his arm and thrust him toward Amanda. "Do me a favor, sweet pea, and dance with Amanda. Believe me, it's the only chance you'll get, because she'll be mobbed as soon as she gets out on the dance floor."

"It will be my pleasure." Wilford adjusted his glasses and swung Amanda into his arms. He held her carefully, like a Dresden doll, guiding her across the crowded floor, dancing with more enthusiasm than expertise.

Tanner saw them coming. As a matter of fact, he'd watched every move Amanda had made since she'd entered the room. Even after he'd walked away from her, pretending not to care, he'd watched her. When she'd thrown back her head, laughing in that full-throated, uninhibited way she had, he'd been jealous that he hadn't been the cause of her joy. Damn the woman, he thought, cursing to himself. The day before, he'd believed he could drive away and forget her, but he'd been wrong. She was still a fever in his blood, and he had to have her, even if it meant making a complete spectacle of himself in his hometown. That would certainly be nothing new. Shifting Evelyn Jo to get a better view of Amanda, he chuckled.

"What's so funny, Tannah?" Evelyn Jo's exaggerated accent was so thick, he could almost see it dripping from her mouth. If she hadn't been such a good sport, he would have regretted his hasty choice of a substitute.

"I was just thinking how good it is to be home for Christmas, Evelyn Jo." Out of the corner of his eye he noticed that Amanda had changed dance partners already. Good. He didn't want one man to have his hands on her too long.

"We'ah always so *dehlighted* to have you home."

"Tell me, Evelyn Jo, is Riverside Church having its annual Christmas cantata tomorrow night?"

"What a strange thing to be askin'."

"I like to sing." Amanda and her partner were dancing so close to them now that he could smell her perfume. She used to put her fragrance on every pulse point of her body. He remembered what fun he'd had tracing the scent and kissing every spot. He felt a sudden jealous urge to toss her partner out the window.

"I remembah. You have a beautiful baritone voice. Of course they are. It's tradition, you know."

Now, what the hell was Evelyn Jo babbling about? he wondered. Then he remembered. "Amanda always used to sing the lead soprano part," he said casually. "Now that she's back in town, I don't suppose she's singing at Riverside again."

"Why, as a mattah of fact, she is. She's doin' that part tomorrah. It made old Corinne Luckett madder than hell, if you'll pahdon the expression. She fancies herself the best voice in the Delta. The rest of us are tickled to death to have Amanda back. We'ah tired of Corinne's screechin'."

Tanner threw back his head and roared. One of the things he missed most about living in Dallas was the small-town intrigue. As he laughed, he caught Amanda staring at him. He winked. She merely arched her perfect eyebrows and danced on by.

"I think Riverside is going to have a new voice in its choir tomorrow."

"Why, Tannah. You don't even know the music."

"I'm a quick study. Especially with a good teacher like you."

Evelyn Jo laughed. "I can take a hint, Tannah Donovan. But if you dare tell anybody you spent the night at my house practicin' for the church choir, I'll call you the biggest liah in the Delta."

"Evelyn Jo, you can tell them anything you want, and I'll vow and declare it's true."

"Then get ready to have your reputation enhanced, Tannah Donovan."

Leaning down, he kissed her cheek. It gave him wicked pleasure to see that Amanda shot him a murderous look. "You're a real sport, Evelyn Jo."

"I'm also dyin' to get my hot little hands on that ex-husband of mine. Would you mind dancin' that way and sort of droppin' me off? Dancin' with you, I think I've made him jealous enough to rouse his interest."

"Why, Evelyn Jo. I do believe you're a devious woman."

"No more devious than you, Tannah. Ever'body heah saw the way you kissed Amanda."

He grinned. "I never did learn to be subtle." He maneuvered them across the floor and released her. "Save the last dance for me."

Evelyn Jo winked. "It's a date, you big gorgeous hunk of man." She blew him a kiss, then put a special hitch in her size-twelve hips as she walked toward her ex-husband.

Tanner turned swiftly back to the dance floor, his gaze searching out Amanda. She was near the French doors that led to the courtyard, being held much too close by her third dance partner. Being in the same room with her this long and not holding her again would be negligent, stupid, and downright sinful, Tanner decided as he strode toward her.

He loved the way her eyes widened when he tapped her partner on the shoulder. "Do you mind if I cut in?"

After Amanda had been relinquished to him, he pulled her close and leaned down to whisper, "Do you think we'll get arrested for what we've been doing?"

"And what is that, Tanner?" Her voice was cool and controlled, but he could feel the wild thumping of her heart against his chest.

He pulled back and smiled triumphantly at her. "Making love in public."

"You're insane."

"I saw the way you watched me."

"I didn't—"

"Just as I watched you," he said, interrupting her smoothly. "It was in your eyes, Amanda. The lovemaking. Remember how it used to be?"

"No." He knew she was lying. The racing of her heart told him so.

"All it took was a look between us, that long gaze that was purely sexual. We did it with our eyes, Mandy. Even sitting in old Mrs. Brensley's English class. She never knew that Shakespeare could be so erotic."

"I've read that people often romanticize the past, Tanner."

"Our past doesn't need romanticizing. It merely needs remembering."

"Funny you should say that."

"Why?"

"Aren't you the man who swore to bed me, but not for old times' sake?"

"Yes. But I'll do anything to promote my cause."

"The nostalgia bit won't work."

"Then I'll have to try something else."

He maneuvered smoothly around the dancing couples and through the French doors. Still holding her close, he danced her across the moonlit patio until they were standing under the stone archway that led to the rose garden. One hardy, late-blooming rose sent its fragile fragrance to them on the chill December air.

Without thinking of the consequences, or even caring, Tanner bent down and captured her lips with his. The moment he touched that sweet flesh, he was lost. Gone were his intentions of taking what he wanted without feeling. Forgotten was his resolve to purge his mind and his soul by thoughtless coupling. The woman he held was special. No other woman, before or after Amanda, had ever kissed the way she did. Her spirit was in the kiss, a joyful, exuberant spirit that reached out and touched his very soul.

Against all his carefully laid plans, Tanner found himself kissing her with tenderness and feeling. A thousand remembered kisses replayed themselves as they stood under the pale winter moon. He felt her hands steal around his neck and lace through his hair. He felt the subtle shifting of her hips as they fitted themselves against his in the well-remembered way that used to make him lose all track of time. As the kiss deepened, he was caught up in the rhythmic way she moved against him.

He knew that she was lost too. She could be his for the taking. Soon. Perhaps tonight. He could sense it. Instead of triumph, he felt a strange sort of sadness. Silently cursing himself for a fool, he broke the embrace.

"Now I know, Amanda."

Even in the dim light of the moon he could see the flush on her cheeks. It was disturbingly appealing.

"Know what, Tanner?"

"What works with you." Leaning casually against the stone archway, he studied her. "You like to be dominated."

His words had the calculated effect. She went from flushed uncertainty to towering rage.

"You're an arrogant, frivolous playboy, Tanner Donovan, and I thank my lucky stars that I jilted you."

"You're magnificent when you're angry. You bring the same passion to your rages that you do to your bed."

"Is that all you think about?"

"Yes. My needs are very elemental. A little food, adequate shelter, plenty of sex, and I'm a happy man."

"I'm glad I married Claude. Lord, I'd hate to think what life with you would have been like."

"Fun." He rammed his hands in his pockets to keep from reaching out and dragging her back into his arms. "By the way, if you're so glad you married Claude, why did you leave him?"

"It had nothing to do with you."

He wondered if she were lying and what difference it would make.

"I think it's a habit you have, Amanda—loving and leaving. But this time it'll be different. I'm the one who will do the leaving."

He turned away from her quickly, before he could change his mind. And as he left her there on the moonlight-washed patio, he wondered if her words were prophetic. Would the hunter become the hunted?

Three

Amanda was late, and it was all Tanner's fault. If it hadn't been for him, she'd have gotten a decent night's rest; then she wouldn't have fallen asleep on her sofa in the afternoon.

She parked her car and headed toward the Riverside Church. The choir room was empty when she arrived. Grabbing her robe off its hook, she hastily slipped it over her dress and started for the choir loft. The rest of the members were assembled in the hall, waiting to go inside the sanctuary.

Still fumbling with her collar, she picked her way through the crowd. "Excuse me," she said as she edged around a very tall man.

"Do you need any help with that?"

She jerked her head up and looked into the twinkling eyes of Tanner Donovan.

"What are you doing here?"

"I was planning to sing . . . unless you have something else in mind."

What she had in mind couldn't be discussed in church, she thought. She still could feel the bruising crush of his lips on hers. Just looking at him made her want more, but she'd never let him know it.

"Behave yourself. You're in church."

"I was always naughty in church." He reached up and straightened her collar, letting his hand linger on the nape of her neck. "You did know how to dress in a hurry, Amanda."

She felt a quick rush of heat through her body. If she didn't get away from him soon, she'd be doing things in the back of the church that would be fodder for another Donovan-Lassiter legend. Striving to get herself in the proper frame of mind, she stepped back.

"Unhand me, unless you plan to follow me to the front and sing soprano."

"No. I prefer to sit behind you, so I can enjoy the view."

She couldn't think of a feisty comeback; her mind was too busy cataloging the wicked charms of Tanner Donovan. Fortunately the line began to move and she was forced to hurry into place with the sopranos. Otherwise she might have done something that would make even the most liberal-minded Southerners blush.

As she hurried forward she wondered what in the devil Tanner was doing there in a choir robe, and whether he actually intended to sing. She wouldn't put anything past him. Especially after the previous night. He had a magnificent voice, but he hadn't been in town long enough to attend a single practice. He had probably come only to sit back there and aggravate her.

Amanda slid into her seat, acutely aware of the moment Tanner sat down directly behind her. As the organ prelude swelled, filling the church with magnificent sound, she knew she was supposed to be thinking exalted thoughts, but the only thing that came to her mind was body heat. Tanner's body heat. It reached out and seared her.

She was playing a dangerous game with Tanner Donovan, she thought, a game that might have no winners. But Fate had dealt the cards, and she would play the hand. Win, lose, or draw, she was in the game for the duration. With that last irreverent thought she turned her attention back to the service. She was here to sing, and nothing would stop her. Not even Tanner Donovan.

Determination always brought out the best in Amanda. From the moment the music started, she was in fine voice. Even when Tanner's rich baritone voice joined in, hers never faltered. The goose bumps popped up on her arm, as they always had when he sang, but she ignored them. For an instant she wondered how he'd ever learned the cantata, but she didn't have time to ponder that. Fleetingly she noticed how well their voices blended, but she didn't have time to think about that, either. Nothing would mar her singing.

She lifted her voice with renewed determination, making the beautiful old Gothic church ring with glorious music.

When it was all over, the congregation flocked to the front to congratulate the choir.

"That was wonderful, Amanda." Maxine managed to hem her in behind the altar rail with Tanner. "You two perform so well together." Wilford, who was standing as close to Maxine as he thought prudent in church, nodded his agreement.

"I always thought so." Tanner moved in close and put his hand on Amanda's shoulder. To the innocent bystander the gesture was completely harmless. Only she knew that he had his thigh pressing against the back of her choir robe. Nor did she miss the double meaning of his words. She'd lay bets that he wasn't talking about singing.

Over her shoulder she shot him a look that would have made a lesser man quail. Tanner winked at her.

Maxine's next words only encouraged him. "The two of you should perform together more often."

"Those are my intentions," Tanner said.

"Over my dead body." Amanda considered murder, with a hymnal right there in the church.

Maxine was in her element. She loved controversy, especially when she was right in the middle of it. "I have the most wonderful idea. Wilford and I always go to Jimmy's for coffee after church. Why don't you two join us?"

"Great, we'd love to. Jimmy's is one of our favorite places," Tanner said.

"No, thank you," Amanda said at the same time, but nobody paid any attention.

"Good. Then it's settled. We'll wait for you to shuck the robes, and we'll all go in my car. It's more fun being together, don't you think?"

Wilford finally managed to get a word in edgewise. "Maxine is such a wonderful manager."

Amanda decided she would wait until tomorrow to tell Maxine what she was—a dyed-in-the-wool mischief maker.

"Amanda and I will be right back." Tanner took her arm and steered her toward the choir room. "Are you ready to get undressed, darling?"

She saw that she was trapped. Being cornered always brought out her fighting spirit. She could play the game as well as he. "Certainly. And I do enjoy an audience."

"Have you ever lacked for one?"

So, she thought, the bold and brash Tanner Donovan wasn't without feelings. That question smacked of jealousy if she'd ever heard it. She decided to add fuel to the fire.

"Never. I've lost count since Claude."

She saw the fleeting look of rage on his face before he recovered. "Good for you. I love an experienced woman."

"I thought love didn't enter into this."

"It doesn't. That was a general statement."

"Good. I'd hate to think you were having second thoughts about this game, just when I'm starting to enjoy it."

As she pushed open the door and entered the empty choir room, she began to have second thoughts about her own game tactics. Tanner in a crowd was one thing; Tanner alone was quite another. But he was right behind her; it was too late to back out now. She walked quickly across the room, putting as much space between them as possible.

She heard the metallic click of a zipper. Although she knew it was only his choir robe, she had visions of other times when she'd heard that same sound. Her cheeks flushed as she remembered the times she'd turned to find Tanner standing beside her, magnificent in his nakedness.

There was no going back, she reminded herself. All she could do was move ahead. The faster, the better. She needed to put Tanner out of her life. Now was no time for cowardice.

"I always seem to have trouble with zippers." She turned and walked boldly toward him. "If I remember correctly, you're an expert with these."

"I've had a lot of practice." He put his hands on her shoulders and gently brought her closer.

"So I've read." Now it was her turn to hurt. She didn't like to think of him with other women. She didn't want any reminders that the hands grasping her so tenderly had done the same thing countless times over the years—but to someone else. She just wouldn't think about that, she decided. Such thoughts were dangerous.

His hands felt so good. Whenever he had touched her, she had experienced an immediate sense of well-being, as if nothing in the world could harm her as long as Tanner was there. And now, standing in the choir room, that old feeling threatened to overwhelm her again.

In a flash of hindsight she realized that coming here with him had been a mistake, one that she would remedy quickly. She pushed his hands away and stepped back. "I won't be added to your long list of conquests."

"I thought you loved an audience."

"Not this audience."

"I'm devastated. Perhaps I should get my minister to send you a letter of recommendation."

"I doubt that a man of your reputation has more than a nodding acquaintance with men of the cloth."

Tanner laughed. It was a full-bodied, deep-throated sound of pure delight. "Don't let Paul hear you say that. He's worked for ten years to tame the hellion in me."

"If I remember correctly, your older brother was quite a hellion himself."

He laughed even harder. "I can't wait to tell him how you remember him. It'll be good for the Reverend Paul Donovan to hear that."

Amanda loved getting news about Paul. She'd always liked Tanner's brothers, especially Paul and Theo, but she was determined not to be side-tracked. "It's a good thing he has God on his side. And even so, I have my doubts about his taming you." She put her hands on her hips and gazed at him boldly. "Tanner Donovan, you're every inch the hellion."

"I don't deny that." With one step he closed the space between them. "Come here, Mandy, love. This hellion is dying to get into your zipper."

Before she could protest, his hands were on her, the left holding her shoulder while the right slowly lowered her zipper. She'd never known that shedding a choir robe could be such a sensuous experience. His fingers trailed the path of the zipper, brushing across her clothes, lingering intimately over her breasts. She felt the heat of his hand through the silk of her blouse.

She held her breath as the zipper inched downward. He made no move to come closer. He made no attempt to embrace her. The only change was in his eyes. She saw the bright light of passion gleaming in their quicksilver depths.

Willing herself not to respond, she stood very still as he worked his magic. His left hand continued to hold her shoulder, while the right explored her body behind the widening path of the zipper. She felt a tiny bead of nervous perspiration roll between her breasts as the zipper skimmed below her waist.

"You used to love this, Mandy." Her skirt was no protection from the touch of his fingers. Lazily he was drawing those familiar erotic circles that used to drive her wild.

"Not anymore." With a supreme effort she controlled her breathing, but there was nothing she could do about the thundering of her heart. She hoped he didn't hear it in the still of the choir room.

"You still do. I can tell."

She thought his laughter was positively diabolical.

"You're a wicked man, Tanner Donovan. I don't know why I ever fell in love with you."

He quickly finished opening her robe and slipped it from her shoulders.

"I do. If we weren't in church, I'd show you."

"After all these years you've developed scruples?"

"Are you disappointed?"

"No. Surprised." She took the robe from his hand and hung it up. "And relieved."

"The next time opportunity knocks, we won't be in a church, Amanda."

"Lately I've become hard of hearing."

"I'll see that opportunity knocks loud enough for you to hear." He lifted her suit jacket from the hook and helped her into it. "Soon, my darling. Very soon."

For a moment Amanda believed the endearment was real. But only for a moment. Deep down she knew it was only a part of the game.

Maxine and Wilford were waiting for them in the parking lot. "Hurry, kids," Maxine yelled. "My chariot awaits." She swept her arm toward her Volkswagen Beetle.

"Why don't we take my car?" Amanda suggested. "We'll be crowded in yours."

"That's the general idea." Maxine grinned. "Climb in the back, kids. Once I get the old rattletrap going, there won't be much talking. Who needs to talk, anyhow? It'll be just like old times."

Too much like old times for comfort, Tanner thought as he helped Amanda into the backseat. Everything was getting to be too much like old times—the way Amanda laughed, the way she kissed, the way she felt in his arms. Something inside him was starting to thaw. He didn't want to feel mellow toward her; he wanted to punish her. In one move she'd destroyed their future together and forever separated him from his best friend.

He folded himself into the backseat, lifting Amanda onto his lap.

"Is this necessary?"

"My legs are too long. The only way we'll both fit back here is if you sit on top." He pulled her comfortably into the curve of his arm. "Does it bother you?"

"No more than it bothers you."

As Maxine started up her little Beetle and spun out of the parking lot, he had time to consider just how much holding Amanda did bother him. It felt a lot like being in love, and that wasn't possible. Not anymore. Not with Amanda.

Over the rattle of the old car Maxine yelled something to Amanda about the shop, and she leaned over the seat to reply. That sudden shift of her bottom on his lap left no doubt in either of their minds about her effect on him. She turned her head and lifted a quizzical eyebrow. Shrugging his shoulders, he smiled.

"Opportunity knocking," he murmured.

"Tell opportunity it's not polite to come in without an invitation."

He chuckled. "Tell invitation not to speak so eloquently."

She laughed. Listening to the music of her laughter and watching the play of moonlight over her face and hair, he knew that he couldn't continue the heartless game he was playing. At least not tonight. For this one night only, he was going to forget the past and enjoy the moment.

As Maxine steered her rackety old car into the lot in front of Jimmy's, Tanner laid down the shield and took off his armor.

"Truce, Mandy." He spoke softly, for her ears only. "Let's call the battle off."

"I'm not sure I can trust you."

"You can. I promise."

"For how long?"

"One night only. Tonight."

He'd always known that good boys got rewards, and her smile was proof.

"Agreed."

They followed Maxine and Wilford into Jimmy's to have hot chocolate and talk of ordinary things—football and politics and Christmas and Hong Kong. They discussed world peace and small-town morality. They reminisced over their days at Greenville High, and Tanner even told Wilford of the time he and Claude and Amanda had stolen their biggest rival's mascot, a billy goat, and smuggled it into the principal's office. The goat had created such havoc that school had been canceled. Wilford, who was from Chicago, observed that that wasn't much reason to dismiss school. Maxine explained that he didn't know the goat, and Tanner assured him that Southerners were unique. It didn't take much to excite them.

He was thinking mostly of himself when he'd made the remark. He'd been in the finest restaurants in New York, Madrid, Paris, and Hong Kong. But right now, sitting in Jimmy's watching Amanda, he couldn't remember when he'd been more excited. He felt as if he'd just carried the ball fifty yards and crossed the goal line.

It was late when they returned to the church to pick up their cars. As Tanner watched Amanda drive off into the night he vowed that the next day would be different. He wouldn't allow his feelings to get in the way. He'd finish what he'd set out to do.

Tanner woke up quickly, brightly alert, cheerful, his body like a well-oiled machine, fine-tuned and ready to go. The smell of gingerbread and the sound of his mother's singing drifted up the stairs to him. He could hear his father's big boom of laughter, the banging of the front door, and the happy chatter of young voices—some of the Donovan grandchildren coming in to breakfast. For a moment he lay on the feather mattress in the big four-poster bed and listened to the sounds of home. Then he dressed and hurried down to join his family.

Anna Donovan was in the kitchen, her neat salt-and-pepper hair pulled into a French twist, and her still-slim figure encased in a ruffled apron. Tanner kissed her on the cheek, lifted her off her feet, and waltzed her around the kitchen.

When he set her back down, she was flushed with pleasure. "Land sakes! A body can't do a speck of work when you're home, Tanner. Always carrying on. You're just like your father." Her wide smile and the twinkle in her blue eyes betrayed her bluff. Besides that, Tanner knew that she adored all the Donovan men, especially Matthew, his father.

He reached over her shoulder and took a huge piece of hot gingerbread off the stove. Taking a big bite, he rolled his eyes heavenward. "I'd kill for your gingerbread."

Anna suppressed her smile. "That's downright sacrilegious. Don't let your brother Paul hear you talking like that."

"When are they arriving?"

"Not till Thursday. He has candlelight services on Wednesday night."

Tanner ate the last of his gingerbread and strad-dled a kitchen chair. "Mom, you're the wisest woman I know."

Hands on her hips, she turned around to face him. "The last time you said that to me, you had just set the barn on fire."

Tanner laughed. "I was only ten, and it was an accident."

"A body can't be too careful with you around. What is it this time?"

"If you wanted to be swept off your feet, how would you like it to be done?"

She gave him a keen look. "Did you have some-body particular in mind?"

"Just asking."

"Well, a mother can always hope. Look at Paul. He and Martie are so happy—with the twins and her expecting again. And Theo and Charles and Glover, all with wives and children, are just as contented as pigs in the sunshine."

Tanner chuckled. "I don't want to be a pig in the sunshine. I want to know Pop's courting secrets."

"It's been nearly fifty years, but I remember it like it was yesterday. He came calling in a surrey."

"That old surrey that is still in the barn?"

"That's the one. Matthew rarely used that old Ford he had. He was a terrible driver."

"He still is."

"Don't let your father hear you say that. Any-way, he had the finest pair of matched horses I've ever seen. They were black. He was wearing a white suit and a Panama hat and carrying the biggest box of chocolates I've ever seen. I fell in love with him on the spot."

"Thanks, Mom." Jumping up, he gave her an exuberant kiss, then bounded toward the door.

"Tanner Donovan, where are you going? You haven't even had your breakfast."

"I don't have time. I'm going courting."

Amanda had taken advantage of the Monday morning lull in business to climb into her shop window and set up a new display. She heard the commotion on Washington Street a mere second before Maxine raced toward the door.

"Good Lord! Amanda, look at that."

Leaving the mannequin half naked, she walked to the front of her window and looked out. There, dressed in a white cowboy suit, white boots, and the biggest white ten-gallon hat she'd ever seen, was Tanner Donovan. He was sitting in an ancient surrey with faded fringe on the top, and beside him was a foil-wrapped box nearly as big as he was. The surrey was pulled by an ornery, slow-moving old mule, and traffic was backed up behind him for two blocks. But nobody seemed to mind. Folks were hanging out of their car windows, cheering and whistling; and Lard Pritchard, the Washington Street traffic cop, was tooting his whistle, waving his white-gloved hands at the gathering crowd on the sidewalk and grinning as if it were already Christmas.

Amanda hooted with laughter.

The surrey drew to a stop directly in front of her shop. Tanner stepped down, stood in front of her window, and swept off his hat.

"Madame, I've come to sweep you off your feet."

"Tanner Donovan, you've tried tricks before. I'm not budging from this window."

"In that case I'll have to carry you."

The crowd cheered as he rammed his ten-gallon hat back onto his head and strode into her shop.

Four

Amanda stood staunchly in her window, but the minute Tanner entered her shop, she felt as if she'd been pulled into the middle of cyclone. She was determined that he wouldn't know it. Putting the mannequin between them, she laughed. "You look ridiculous in that hat."

Tanner tipped his hat back and smiled up at her. "I was hoping for irresistible."

"You missed it by a country mile."

"Then why are you hiding behind that dummy?"

"I'm not hiding." She quickly busied her hands draping the mannequin in an antique ruby silk dress. "I'm dressing this poor naked creature."

"I'd offer to help, but I'm better at undressing."

"No doubt."

He closed in, trapping her in the window. "I've come to take you for a buggy ride, Amanda."

"I'm not going."

"I'll make you change your mind."

"Not till hell freezes over."

"Madame, hell is about to freeze over." He planted one white boot on the display window. Amanda felt the floor shake under his weight.

"Are you crazy?"

"Yes."

"Get your big feet out of my window before the whole thing falls down."'

"My granddaddy built this store. It can withstand a hurricane. Say yes, Amanda."

"Never!"

Another huge white boot came into view, and while her mouth was still forming words of protest, Tanner stepped onto the window platform with her.

Outside, the crowd cheered. Inside, Maxine let out a rebel yell.

"Hot damn, Tanner! We haven't had this much excitement around here since the mayor's wife lost her half slip at the Fourth of July picnic."

Amanda glared at her over the top of the mannequin. "You and Nero would have made quite a team, Maxine. You stand there cheering, and I'm about to lose my life in this rickety display window."

"I was thinking more in terms of your virtue." In two bold moves Tanner pushed the mannequin aside and pulled Amanda into his arms. Another cheer went up from the crowd pressed around the window, and Maxine let out a dramatic stage sigh.

As Tanner bent closer, Amanda saw the twins sparks of mischief and desire in his eyes. "You wouldn't dare."

"Wouldn't I?"

He was so close, she could feel the warmth of his breath against her cheek. Her thighs felt scorched where they touched his. Before she could be seduced by Tanner, she regained her fighting spirit.

"The first time you took my virtue, we didn't have an audience."

She felt his arms slacken, saw the indecision flit briefly across his face. It was a small moment of triumph, a reminder that their past could not be forgotten—nor forgiven.

She pressed her advantage. "I have work to do. You'll have to find another companion for your buggy, and whatever else you have in mind. Why don't you ask Evelyn Jo?"

"Jealous, Amanda?"

His mischievous grin reminded her of the time he'd let a bullfrog loose in the auditorium during Parents' Day.

"Certainly not. I'm glad you've found another recipient for your wicked charms."

"Do you find me charming?"

She found him so charming that she was in danger of making a complete fool of herself right in her own display window. Somehow the game she was playing didn't seem to be working right. Seeing Tanner was supposed to disenchant her, not confuse her, and certainly not seduce her. It was time to end the game.

"You lost your charm long ago, Tanner, when you chose a pigskin over me. I much prefer the steady attraction of a man like Claude to that will-o'-the-wisp behavior you call charm."

Tanner's eyes blazed as he reached out and scooped her up into his arms. He held her so hard against his chest, she could barely breathe.

"Claude isn't here for you to run to, Amanda. It's just you and me."

"Put me down!"

There was no humor in his smile. "Afraid?"

"Not of the devil. And certainly not of you."

"You should be."

The window shook as he stepped down, clutching Amanda tightly against his chest.

"You pirate. Where are you going?"

"On a picnic. You'll love it."

"I have a shop to run."

Tanner turned to Maxine. "Can you handle the shop by yourself today?"

"Don't you dare say yes," Amanda warned.

Maxine fluffed up her blond hair and grinned. "I can handle this shop even if a herd of buffalo come stampeding in here. You two go on and have fun."

"Fun!" Amanda's angry retort was lost in the tinkling of the shop's bell as Tanner opened the door.

He turned back to Maxine. "Thanks, doll. I owe you."

"You can send me an outrageously expensive wedding gift."

"I'll do more than that. I'll pay for the honeymoon."

"Well, hot damn."

"It's a conspiracy," Amanda muttered as Tanner strode boldly onto the street.

The townspeople, who had waited around for the finale, clapped and cheered, then scattered to go on about their Christmas errands.

"The whole town must be in on this."

"Haven't you read the papers? I'm their favorite native son. They love me."

"Well, I don't."

"Good. That means nobody will be hurt this time."

They glared at each other. Amanda was shocked at what she saw in his eyes. Remnants of pain. She recognized it because she'd seen it in her own eyes too often not to know. A tiny glow of hope flickered to life inside her. Was it possible, she wondered, that after eleven years a part of Tanner still loved her as she did him? After everything they'd done to each other, could they have a second chance?

The warm December breeze lifted a strand of her hair and brushed it gently against his cheek.

She saw the softening of his expression. It almost resembled love.

Her hand trembled as she reached up to touch his familiar square jaw. The moment took on a brilliant clarity. Each note of the Christmas music drifting from the stores was joyful and hauntingly sweet. The chatter of the Christmas shoppers added a gay counterpoint to the music. Even the timid rattle of dry leaves in the old oak beside her shop, and the scolding of a gray city squirrel added to the beautiful melody that was playing around her. Lard Pritchard's whistle marked the time.

Her fingertips brushed his face, hesitantly, tenderly. He leaned close to her, so close that their breath mingled. She could almost taste his lips. Her tongue drew a tiny circle around her mouth.

Tanner closed his eyes and let out a harsh breath. Pulling back, he stared into her face.

"How am I doing, Amanda? Is this the kind of courtship you like? Is this what it takes to get you into my bed?"

The hand that had been caressing his face drew back and slapped him. "You frivolous playboy. You'll never get me into your bed. Never!"

"If that little love pat is all the fight you're going to put up, I've got this touchdown as good as made." He walked with confidence and arrogance as he crossed the sidewalk and placed her in the surrey.

"You never could get your mind off football for long, could you, Tanner?" She gave the enormous, foil-wrapped box a vicious kick. "If you think I'm here against my will, you're sadly mistaken. I'm going on this damned buggy ride so I can verify all the reasons I jilted you in the first place. Every minute I spend with you confirms the wisdom of marrying Claude."

She'd waved the red flag, and she knew it. It

gave her a malicious satisfaction to see the tight-
ening of his jaw.

"If Claude was so damned wonderful, why aren't
you still married to him?" The surrey creaked as
he stepped in.

"I'm not about to swap bedroom tales with you."

"Claude wasn't any good in bed?"

Tanner snapped the reins and got the old mule
into motion.

"I didn't say that. As a matter of fact, Claude
was—"

"I didn't ask for the gory details." Tanner's voice
was harsh as he cut her off.

Amanda felt a small surge of triumph that she'd
touched a nerve, but it didn't compensate for the
death of a dream. Apparently fate had never meant
for the two of them to love. Tanner's negligence
eleven years before, and his coldness now, made
that achingly clear to her. As the mule clopped
slowly down the street and they sat side by side in
icy silence, she was grateful that Christmas wouldn't
last forever. Soon it would be over and Tanner
would go back to Dallas. Until then she'd endure.
She'd meet every one of his outrageous tactics
with fire and spirit. She'd use him, just as he was
using her. Catharsis was the name of the game.
Each time she was with Tanner, she'd take mental notes of his shortcomings. People didn't change.
The man sitting beside her was the same man
she'd once jilted—and with good cause. She'd keep
reminding herself of that until she was convinced.

They were almost on the outskirts of town before Tanner spoke.

"You took back your maiden name."

"Yes."

"Why?"

"Is it important?"

He turned and gazed at her a long time before

answering. "Everything about you is important." Tanner saw the beginnings of her beautiful smile. It shook his resolve to bed her and leave her. He almost changed his mind.

"Is it?" Her soft inquiry felt like nails driven through his heart.

"Yes," he wanted to say. But the empty years and the remembered pain got in the way.

"Certainly." He turned his attention back to keeping the old mule on a straight course to the river. Not looking at Amanda helped him play out the deceit. "The way to win is to know your opponent."

"Life is a big game to you, isn't it, Tanner?"

"Is that what you thought when you left me?"

"I didn't leave you. You left me."

"I'd hardly call going to Alabama on a football scholarship leaving you. Besides, I was there when you came over to visit."

"After all these years you still don't understand, do you?"

"I tried, Amanda. Heaven knows I tried."

"You were there physically, Tanner, but Claude is the one I had to depend on. When we'd leave Southern University on the weekend and drive over to see you, nine times out of ten we'd have to wait in line behind your coach, your football teammates, your fans, and the press."

"You knew how I felt about football before you agreed to marry me."

"I guess I really didn't know until your last year in college. When you broke Joe Namath's passing record, made All-SEC, and won the Heisman Trophy, you became a public property. I wanted a husband, Tanner, and a real home—and children."

"I love children. We would have had them."

"When? During time-outs at football games?"

"I'd forgotten how stubborn you are, Amanda. It's a damn good thing we didn't marry."

"Right. With your pigheadedness . . ."

"And your sassy tongue . . ."

"And your high-handed ways . . ."

"And your slave-driver approach to work . . ."

"Don't forget your frivolity . . ."

"Not to mention your redheaded temper . . ."

They both burst out laughing. The old mule slowly turned his head to see what all the commotion was about. Seeing nothing but two happy people, he continued his poky pace to the river.

When they had stopped laughing, Tanner reached over and took her hand.

"Mandy, I'm completely out of the mood to seduce you."

"What a relief. I'm out of the mood to fight with you."

"Good. What do you say we run up the white flag and enjoy the rest of the day."

"Agreed. How long is this truce going to last, Tanner?"

"At least all day. Maybe even two days. I guess I'm feeling the Christmas spirit."

"And I'm feeling enormously hungry. Did you bring a picnic lunch?"

"I was so busy convincing old Josephine to pull this surrey and getting the candy that I guess I forgot."

"Chocolate?"

He grinned. "Yes. I remembered your sweet tooth."

"Well, don't keep me waiting. Where is it?"

"It's in that big box you kicked."

Amanda leaned down and ripped off the foil wrapping. "If I've destroyed one precious bite of chocolate, I'm going to be devastated." She pulled out a Hershey bar with almonds, tore into the wrapper, and took a big bite. "Ummmm. Delicious." She took another bite and rolled her eyes heavenward. "I'd die for candy."

"You'd live on it if somebody didn't remind you to eat right. Who does that now, Mandy?"

"Maxine. She plays mother hen to me all the time."

"I'll have to remember to thank her." Tanner chuckled as he watched her reach into the box and attack another candy bar. He loved the way she nibbled the almonds, bit by tiny bit, savoring every piece. He never knew he'd be jealous of a chocolate bar. "What about me? Don't I get one little bite?"

She leaned over and pressed a half-eaten bar into his mouth. He took his time, savoring the feel of her hand on his shoulder, the look of sunlight in her eyes, and the touch of her fragrant hair brushing against his cheek. He knew the sweetness he tasted was from her lips and not the candy.

"Enough?" she asked.

"I'll never get enough."

"Nor will I."

Their breathing became harsh as his eyes asked, hers said yes, and they were caught up in the spell. Quicksilver and sun-kissed blue—searching, hungry, passionate, yielding. It was so like old times that the years of emptiness might never have been between them.

Amanda was the first to pull away. She scooted back to her side of the surrey. They were both trembling.

"I was talking about chocolate."

"So was I."

She figured one more lie wouldn't hurt, and he figured Santa was going to leave a lump of coal in his stocking, anyway.

Tanner decided his sanity hinged on getting to

the river. He'd always felt right in the presence of the Mississippi, at peace, somehow in tune with the elements of nature.

"Look. There it is, Amanda. The river." He pointed as they rounded a bend in the road. "It takes your breath away, doesn't it?"

"Yes. I'm glad we decided not to fight. It would have spoiled everything."

"I've always like that about you, Mandy. You're a woman with a healthy appreciation of nature and the good sense to recognize a beautiful moment."

Tanner guided the surrey off the road and stopped underneath a cypress tree. He helped her down, his hands spanning her small waist. She felt soft and feminine and right. A sense of déjà vu swept over him. Still holding her, he closed his eyes and absorbed the fragrance of her—jasminy, sweet, sultry, and seductive, blending with the fertile smells of the sleeping winter earth and the pulsing river.

He opened his eyes and saw a lovely vulnerability in her face. Lord, she would be so easy to love again. It was something he wouldn't think about right now. Today he would enjoy the moment.

"May I have this dance?"

She put her hands on his shoulders. "Delighted, Tanner."

They danced beside the river, Tanner humming their favorite Gershwin tune, sunlight warming their skin, contentment warming their hearts.

" 'Someone to Watch Over Me.' I haven't thought of that song for years, Tanner."

He loved the huskiness of her voice, the way the sunlight gilded her skin, the way she fit perfectly against him, as if she and she alone were designed to be there.

"Sing with me, Mandy, love."

Their voices lifted in beautiful harmony. It was

a perfect beginning for a perfect day beside the river. They danced until they had exhausted their repertoire of Gershwin songs. Then Tanner spread a quilt under the cypress tree and they stretched out in the sunshine to watch the river traffic. Their talk was lazy and contented, two old friends catching up on the small details of their separate lives. They skirted the painful issues, careful not to mar the tranquillity by any mention of Claude. They talked about Amanda's antique shop and Tanner's latest venture, a chain of restaurants. She asked about the Donovan Home for Children he'd founded, and he asked about the Legacy for Learning she'd helped organize in Fulton.

As the sun climbed higher, they shed their light-weight sweaters and rolled up their sleeves.

"Feel that sunshine, Amanda."

"Umm. Delicious."

"Almost like summer."

"Yes, but with a little nip in the air."

"God's endorsing this picnic."

"It's a pity He didn't remind you to bring real food." She laughed as she reached for another Hershey bar.

"That's seven. You're going to be sick."

"It'll be on your conscience."

"Upsy-daisy." He took her hands and pulled her to her feet.

"Where are we going?"

"Jogging. If we don't burn some of that sugar out of your system, you're going to turn into a sugar cube."

"I hate jogging."

"I remember." He picked her up and raced along the river. "See. It's not so bad."

Her face was rosy from sunshine and laughter. "Not as long as you're doing all the work."

"That was only temporary, madame." He kissed

her flushed cheek and set her on her feet. "Tomorrow I'm going to hate myself for letting you go, but I can't have the ruination of that beautiful body on my conscience." He patted her bottom. "Now march, madame."

"Slave driver." She started a slow trot beside him.

"That's it. One foot in front of the other."

"Slow down, Tanner."

"You can do it. Pick up your speed. Get the old heart pumping."

"This is torture."

"It's great."

"I hate it."

"I love it."

"I intend to complain every breath."

"You're doing a wonderful job of that."

"Do you do this every day?"

"Yes. At least six miles a day."

"If you think I'm going six miles, you're crazy."

"Just to that oak tree up ahead."

"That's a thousand miles away, Tanner."

"It's more like a thousand feet."

"My feet hurt. I've stepped on forty-five rocks, and my shoes aren't made for running."

"Poor baby. Of course they're not. I'm so sorry."

He scooped her up into his arms once more. "There. Is that better?"

She heaved a big sigh of contentment and cuddled against his chest. "Much better. I'm so glad I came today. I never realized how totally unsuited to each other we are."

He stood gazing into her face, thinking that he'd never really known how totally *suited* to each other they were. Amanda, at eighteen, had been bright and beautiful and charming. At thirty-three, she was all that and more, so much more. She had a quick wit and a warm personality and a breathtaking sensuality. Being with her was like having Christmas shining in his soul.

"Yes. Totally unsuited." His voice was soft, husky, blending with the gentle murmur of the river. "I always loved the way your eyes look in the sunlight, Mandy. There's a little pot of gold right in the center of all that beautiful blue-green." He bent closer.

She touched his face, letting her fingertips play tenderly along his cheeks and around his jaw. "Your face, Tanner. I could never forget the strong lines, those wonderful cheekbones, and that square, stubborn jaw."

He bent so close that their lips were almost touching. "Since we both agree . . ." His tongue drew a lazy circle around her mouth.

She sighed. ". . . that we're a mismatch."

"It would be sinful not to kiss you."

"A waste."

There was a terrible hunger in their kiss. Like starving lovers too long denied, they devoured each other. They clung together, their soft cries of pleasure muffled against each other's lips. The love that they so stoutly denied came pouring forth in the kiss.

Tanner lowered Amanda's feet to the ground, sliding her down his body, branding himself with the glorious feel of her. He buried his left hand in her hair and moved his right to cup her buttocks. He reveled in the perfect fit of her hips against his, marveled at the sensations that rocked him.

He plunged his tongue deep into her mouth, thrusting in perfect imitation of love. She arched against him, and he didn't know who started it first, but suddenly their hips were moving, rotating in a sensuous abrasion that nearly shattered his control.

He wanted to take her right there beside the

river, with the winter sun warming their skin. He wanted to strip off her clothes and taste every gorgeous inch of her body. Desire rose in him so strongly that he thought he would explode.

"Mandy . . ." The word was half plea, half groan, spoken against her lips.

"Tanner . . . please."

As their mouths continued their hungry course, the rhythm of their hips increased, and he knew that Amanda was as blinded by passion as he. They were on the cutting edge of danger, about to plunge over. One more minute of this sweet agony and there would be no turning back for him. He'd have Amanda—in every way. But it wouldn't be the end, it would be the beginning; the beginning of madness.

It took every ounce of control he possessed to pull away from her. Looking at her, flushed with desires was as gut-wrenching as kissing her. He almost took her—the consequences be damned.

"That's a good way to end a picnic." Years of courage under pressure allowed him to hold his hands steady as he brushed her tumbling hair back from her face. "A simple kiss, no feelings involved."

"Absolutely none."

How he loved her courage! She was perfectly poised, meeting his gaze with a cool, steady one that belied her high color and kiss-pouted mouth. He wanted to haul her back into his arms and take her so fiercely, so thoroughly, that she would be bound to him forever. He wanted to enslave her with passion so that she would *never* turn to another man.

He reached out and cupped her face. "Mandy?"

He wanted to drown in those beautiful eyes she lifted to him. "What is it, Tanner?"

Temptation ripped through him, and he almost

gave in. But he knew, looking down at her, that he would be the one enslaved. Taking her again wouldn't be release; it would be bondage.

He lowered his hands, vowing to himself again that tomorrow would be different. "Time to go home."

"Yes. I feel guilty leaving Maxine alone in the shop so long. It is the Christmas season, you know."

He took her hand as they walked toward the surrey. "I'll help out, Amanda—to make up for taking you away from the shop. I've never sold antique ladies' clothing, but I can learn."

She laughed. "I can just see you among all those ruffled petticoats and tiny pearl buttons. The ladies would love it, of course, but I'm afraid that with that big athlete's body you'd be as out of place as a bull in a china shop. No thanks, Tanner."

They gathered the quilt and the leftover chocolate bars and headed back into town. Progress in the rusty old surrey was slow, but neither of them minded. There was a pleasant camaraderie between them, a comfortable give-and-take that had nothing to do with the past. The image of Amanda that he'd held for eleven years gradually faded under the reality of the Amanda who sat at his side. She was a stunning, mature, multifaceted woman, a woman who was constantly growing and changing, a woman a man would never tire of. He ached for everything he had missed and was missing.

When he left her at the shop, he felt as if there were two minutes left in the game and he'd thrown a touchdown pass that had missed its mark.

"What I need is a hot meal and a restoration of sanity." Talking to the mule seemed ordinary under the circumstances.

He loosened the reins and urged old Josephine homeward.

"If you don't look like the cat that swallowed the canary, I don't know who does." Maxine pulled out a chair and motioned to Amanda. "Sit down and tell me every delicious detail."

Amanda sat down, pulled off her shoes, and rubbed her feet. "How was business today?"

"Business! You want to talk business when I'm dying of curiosity?'"

Amanda quickly surveyed the shop. "I see the red velvet and the black satin dresses are gone. Who bought them?"

"Evelyn Jo bought the red, and a Mrs. David Blasengame from somewhere up north, Milwaukee, or somewhere snowbound and frigid, bought the black. Now quit pretending you don't know what I'm talking about and tell me why you're all pink and flushed and gorgeous and looking like you've had sex."

"Maxine, if you weren't my dearest and oldest friend, I'd fire you on the spot. Furthermore, I'd be offended."

Maxine laughed. "You're too softhearted to fire me, and you're too tolerant to be offended. I love you like a sister, and I know that something happened on that picnic today."

Amanda felt a rush of affection for her friend. Confiding might help ease the burden. She raked her hand through her hair and glanced toward the door to make sure no customers were coming into the shop. "I'm afraid I'm falling in love with Tanner Donovan all over again."

"That's wonderful."

"That's horrible. We've hurt each other before. I don't want to go through that again."

"How do you know it would happen again?"

"I don't know. It's just a risk that I'm not willing to take." She jumped up and began to pace. "Somehow I've got to get Tanner out of my system."

"I hope you have friends in high places."

"Why?"

"From the looks of you, I think that's going to take an act of Congress."

A reply didn't seem necessary. Besides, Amanda thought, what could she say? Maybe Maxine was right. Maybe it would take an act of Congress to get Tanner out of her system. But she was going to try. By George, if it took till this time next year, she was determined to do it.

She went to the back room and began sorting the petticoats she'd found at an auction in Vicksburg.

Tanner had the old surrey as far as Tudberry's two blocks from Amanda's shop when he realized he had to go back. There was something he needed to do—kiss her again. A gentleman always kissed a lady good-bye. He'd been a fool not to take advantage of that delightful custom.

Whistling a perky tune, he turned the surrey around and headed back toward Amanda's. He was halfway there before he became aware of the song he was whistling—"Taking a Chance on Love." He stopped in mid-verse and swore to himself. Damn, he wasn't going to fall in love with the woman again. He merely wanted to kiss her.

Snapping the reins over the mule's back, he urged her forward.

He felt a keen sense of loss when he stepped into the antique shop. Amanda was nowhere in sight.

Maxine made a beeline for him. "Hi there, good-looking. What can I get for you? As if I didn't know." She fluffed her hair and winked.

Tanner chuckled. "Is clairvoyance one of your talents?"

"I don't have to be clairvoyant to know you've come back to see Amanda. Am I right, or what?"

"You're right. When I left her here earlier, there was something I forgot to do."

"She's in the back room, but I'm not so sure she'll be glad to see you. She's trying to get you out of her system."

Tanner knew he should be happy about that news, but he wasn't. Not by a long shot. As a matter of fact, he reacted the same way old Josephine would if she had a burr under her saddle. He got ornery as hell.

"She is, is she? We'll see about that." He barely noticed Maxine's smile of devilish glee as he settled his ten-gallon hat firmly on his head and stalked toward the back room.

Amanda didn't see him at first. She was leaning over a trunk, her slacks stretched across her backside in a way that would set angels to thinking about sin. Tanner leaned against the doorway and took it all in. He remembered every curve and hollow of those hips—and exactly how they felt. Satiny, smooth, and firm. His mouth went dry. Reaching up, he swiped his hand across his brow. Maybe he should have kept on going toward home.

Amanda leaned deeper into the trunk, muttering to herself. Something about "damned puny buttons and froufrou." Tanner wasn't certain what she'd said. Nor did it matter. That last move had outlined her lingerie lines in clear relief. No panty line, merely the imprint of lace high up the side of her thigh. A teddy, he thought. Underneath those slacks she had on a teddy with French-cut sides. He wondered if it was black lace. Sweat beaded his upper lip, and he didn't even bother to wipe it away.

He remembered the first time he'd seen her in a black lace teddy. It had been the summer between their senior year and college, long, lazy days when love seemed their own invention, and the future merely a bright, indefinable light that beckoned to them.

They'd gone down to Biloxi with a group of high-school friends, the sort of outing that marked good-bye to youth and initiation into adulthood. He and the rest of the boys had been deep-sea fishing that day while all the girls had gone shopping. That night, sunburned but still bursting with energy, they'd all gone dancing. Afterward Amanda had come to his room. It hadn't been the first time they'd loved, but it turned out to be one of the most memorable.

Something about her had been different that night, as if she'd cast off the shy vulnerability of a teenager and become a woman. She'd been provocative, sensuous, and incredibly passionate. With the lights turned down low, she'd pushed him into an easy chair and stood before him. Then she'd stripped. The loud thrumming of his heart was the only music she needed. He'd felt certain she heard it.

First she'd taken the pins from her hair ever so slowly, caressing each flaming strand as it fell to her shoulders. At that moment he could have buried himself in her hair and died happy. He remembered how he'd grown large, just looking at her hair. Then she'd slowly unzipped her dress, a bright red taffeta party frock. The sound of the zipper had sent chills through him. When she'd lowered the dress and revealed the black lace teddy underneath, he'd thought he'd burst through his pants.

He'd started toward her then, but she'd held up her hand, stilling him. Not touching her had been sweet agony, but afterward he was glad he'd waited. She'd stepped out of the dress and stood before him, legs apart, hands on her hips, wearing nothing except the black lace teddy, red high heels so sexy that they should have been declared hazardous to his sanity, and a smile.

It was then that he took her, swiftly and thoroughly. Bending her over backward, he'd devoured her mouth. Locked together, he'd guided them to the bed.

It had been one of those unforgettable nights. From that moment on he'd never seen black lace without thinking of her.

Standing in the doorway, watching her bent over the trunk and thinking about that night, he felt himself harden. Wanting her caused physical pain, but he knew he couldn't take her, not even to get her out of his system. Deep inside, he knew that their rejoining would be a thunderous affair. And Maxine was out there in the shop. When the time came, he wouldn't have an audience.

He felt a moan of agony rise in his throat, the pain of denial. Whether he'd given voice to the agony, he didn't know, but suddenly Amanda's back stiffened. She whirled around. Bright spots of color rode high on her cheeks.

"What do you mean, sneaking up on me like that?" She straightened and faced him defiantly.

"I didn't sneak. As a matter of fact, I made quite a bit of noise. You were so engrossed, you didn't hear me."

She pushed her hair back from her forehead, a gesture of frustration he remembered from years gone by.

"Well, why didn't you say something?"

"And spoil all the fun? The view was absolutely entrancing."

Her face flamed even brighter. "Tanner Donovan! That's just like you. Always taking what you want without asking."

"An apt choice of words." Tossing his hat onto a chair, he left the doorway and stalked her. "I want something from you, Amanda, and I've come to get it."

She moved out of his reach, putting the trunk between them. He had the nerve to laugh. She could have screamed.

"Didn't you vow you'd never run from me?"

"I'm not running. I'm merely standing over here until you tell me what you want and until I can decide whether I'll give it to you."

"It's no fun if I have to ask." He feinted a pass, then closed in for a touchdown. Standing behind the trunk with her pinned against his chest, he smiled. "I forgot to kiss you good-bye, Amanda."

"An oversight we could both live with." She shoved against him. "Don't be fooled into thinking that the Hershey bars softened me up. I've made up my mind. I'll resist you or die trying."

"I can think of better ways to die. For instance, this." His mouth crushed down on hers. It wasn't a good-bye kiss, it was an explosive assault.

Determined to hold him off, she struggled briefly in his arms. Then the drugging power of Tanner Donovan took over. She could no more have resisted than she could have flown to Tahiti without a plane. She welcomed him, reveled in him, feasted on him. The incredible joy of being held by him blotted out everything else.

Need flamed in her. She pressed closer, trying to merge her body with his. Vaguely she was aware of soft sounds, whimperings of desire that were her own. He'd know. The thought flitted through her mind. He'd know how much she wanted him, but she didn't care. Nothing mattered at that moment except being in Tanner's arms, being kissed by him.

She absorbed him, the familiar taste of him, fresh and delicious and somehow very masculine; the familiar shape of his mouth, beautifully molded and firm, exactly right for kissing; the familiar feel of him, broad and solid and enduring. Home, she thought. Home is being held next to Tanner's heart.

She felt him pulling back, ending the kiss.

"No." She wound her hands in his hair and pulled his head back down. She didn't care what he thought: She had to have more of him. Something to get her through the rest of the day and the long night ahead.

His lips touched hers again. She could feel the lines of his smile. Let him feel triumphant, she thought. Let him think that he was the victor. She had won too. She was taking what she wanted, and she would walk away in one piece.

His tongue demanded entry to her mouth. She welcomed it with a greedy intensity. Tanner began a lazy, sensuous rhythm, plunging and withdrawing in precise imitation of lovemaking. The sweet, abrasive motion aroused her until she was wild with wanting. She rocked against him, fitting her hips perfectly to his, circling and caressing, seeking to appease the desperate hunger.

The room became steamy with their harsh breathing. Jungle heat, Amanda thought. She and Tanner wanted each other in a basic, primitive way. Whether it had anything to do with love, she didn't know. For her part, perhaps it did. But she knew his intentions. He'd made them plain enough. Love was not what Tanner Donovan wanted.

It was that last thought that made her brave enough to back away from him. She called upon an unknown strength to let him go, then broke away and stood back. "You can go now. I took what I wanted."

He reached out and touched her cheek. She hoped he didn't feel its heat. Like a fever, Tanner was contagious, and she'd forgotten to stay in quarantine.

"You were always especially beautiful after love-making."

"I suppose your enormous ego makes it necessary for you to exaggerate a simple kiss."

His laugh was mocking. "Nothing is simple between us, Amanda." When he removed his hand from her cheek, she felt deprived. "The next time there won't be clothes between us."

He picked up his hat and strode toward the door, then he was gone. Amanda cupped her burning cheeks with her hands and groaned. Getting Tanner out of her system was going to be the hardest thing she'd ever done.

Five

"Tanner Donovan, if you prowl through this kitchen one more time, you're going to wear the floor out."

Anna smiled at him with such fond indulgence that he knew she didn't mind if he wore fifteen floors out. He scooped an apple out of the bowl on the table as he made another circuit through the house. "Exercise." He grinned at her over the apple.

"Pooh! You exercise by running all over the county. Seems to me more like restlessness. Did something happen on that surrey ride you want to talk about?"

"Nothing that I can't forget if I try."

Anna wiped her hands on a towel and reached up to cup her tall son's face. "I want you to be happy."

"I am, Mom. I have everything I need."

"Except somebody to love."

He roared with laughter. "If the Donovan clan were any bigger, I'd have to live two lifetimes in order to get around to loving them all."

"I'm not talking about kinfolk; I'm talking about somebody special." She turned back to her cooking. "It's not my way to meddle, but I don't think you ever got over that Lassiter girl. Land sakes! How you two used to carry on, talking about how Claude would be best man at the wedding, counting the children you'd have. You even said you'd name the first girl after me. I always thought that would be so nice."

He leaned over and pecked her on the cheek. "I find bachelorhood to my liking. You'll just have to settle for adorable me."

She laughed. "You Donovan men. Cocky as the day is long." She dropped the last of the dumplings into the pot. When she turned around, Tanner had started out the door. "Now where are you going? Supper will be ready in a minute."

"Outside. Theo's hellions need some supervision."

"Supervision, my eye. You'll be right in the middle of their games, having more fun than they do."

Tanner winked at his mother. "Don't tell. I'm trying to change my image."

"What image?"

"Will-o'-the-wisp."

He left Anna shaking her head. She'd never understand, he thought. Even he didn't understand. What did it matter after all these years that Amanda had found Claude's steadiness more appealing than his will-o'-the-wispness? What in the hell was a will-o'-the-wisp, anyway? He needed to put that woman out of his mind.

He turned his attention to his nephews. "Hey, Raymond, Kenneth—let's play some ball."

Theo's sons galloped toward him on gangly teenage legs, whooping for joy.

"Hey, Uncle Tanner. Show us that play you made in the Super Bowl."

"Yeah, man. I want to see if you've still got the stuff."

Tanner ruffled their hair. "I'll show you the stuff."

The backyard game held his attention for thirty minutes, thirty blessed minutes during which Amanda didn't invade his mind. Then Kenneth missed a pass. The ball rolled under a holly bush, startling a cardinal into flight. Suddenly Tanner thought of Amanda. It might have been the setting sun shining on the red bird's wing, reminding him of her hair; or it might have been a flash of memory, a rare white Christmas long ago when he and Amanda had seen a flock of cardinals in the snow. Whatever the reason, he knew that he had to see her. Now.

Promising his nephews another game later in the week, he excused himself and went back into the house. It smelled of Anna's chicken and dumplings and spiced pumpkin pie. Tanner knew exactly what to do.

"Hey, Mom. Do you still have that big picnic basket?" He strode around the kitchen, pulling open every cabinet door.

"Land sakes! What are you up to now?"

"I'm going on a rescue mission. Do you have plenty of food, enough for me to share with a friend?"

"You know good and well that I always cook enough to feed everybody in Greenville. Would this friend happen to be the same one you took out in the surrey this morning?"

"Now, Mom. Get that gleam out of your eye. It's not what you're thinking."

"How do you know what I'm thinking?"

He laughed. "Weren't you the one talking about somebody special and wishing for a namesake? I don't want you to be disappointed. This is not that kind of mission."

"Hmm." Anna found the picnic basket and began to stuff it with food. "I hope she has a hearty appetite. I do so like a girl with a hearty appetite."

Tanner placed the basket in the backseat of his Corvette and backed it out the driveway. As he pointed the car toward Amanda's house he pressed the button to let his windows down. The evening air was crisp and invigorating. It smelled of the river and pine trees and rich Delta earth. Strings of colored lights and bright tinsel decorating the neighborhood houses lit his way.

A great warmth filled Tanner's soul. He blamed it on Christmas. As he neared Amanda's house a song filled his heart. He began to whistle. The song was "Someone to Watch Over Me."

Amanda stood in her bare feet, staring into her refrigerator. As usual, she had given only scant thought to food. It appeared that her choices for an evening meal were limited to cheese and pickles, or pickles and whatever happened to be wrapped in a piece of foil. provided it hadn't already turned green.

Just before she had left the shop, Maxine had delivered a stern lecture on the consequences of not eating right. As Amanda looked at her paltry food supply, she wished she'd paid more attention. The seven Hershey bars she'd had for lunch were now only a memory, and she was hungry.

She'd just about settled on the cheese and pickles when the doorbell rang.

"Good evening, madame. I've come to rescue you from starvation."

The minute she saw him, she forgot about putting Tanner Donovan out of her system.

"Tanner! You look good enough to eat."

"So do you." He held up the picnic basket. "Will this do instead?"

"Do I smell Anna's chicken and dumplings?"

"Yes, you do. May I come in, or do you plan to attack them on the front porch?"

"Come in, and don't you dare drop that basket. That woman's an angel. She must be telepathic. My stomach's been sending out hunger signals all evening."

Tanner stepped into the entry hall. "The food is Anna's, the idea is mine. I plan to be handsomely rewarded."

"Good Southern girls always say proper thank-yous."

"I was thinking of improper."

"If I weren't starving, I'd probably show you the door."

Tanner took her arm. "You never could tell a lie. Your beautiful eyes give you away." Leaning down, he circled her lips with his tongue. "You want me as much as I want you."

She stepped back, put her hands on her hips, and looked him straight in the eye. "That's true. If I weren't so hungry, I'd probably have my way with you right here in the hall. As it is, your virtue is safe with me—at least until after the chicken and dumplings."

"I'd advise you to eat plenty. You're going to need all your strength for what I have in mind."

"Promises, promises." She took his arm and led him into her kitchen. He looked so perfect leaning casually against her Aunt Emma's oak butcher-block table, she thought, just the way he used to. She'd have to remember that he wasn't perfect, that love always came second with him.

Turning her back to him, she opened a cabinet and took down a plate. "Have you eaten?"

"No. I brought enough for two."

"Since you're supplying the food, I suppose it would be rude of me not to invite you to stay. Why don't you get the silver? It's in the same place Aunt Emma used to keep it."

She watched as he walked to the correct drawer

without hesitation. Amazing that after eleven years he remembered such a small detail. She wondered what other small details he remembered.

"How is your Aunt Emma? Mom said that she's in a nursing home now."

"Yes. When my parents moved to Nashville, they took her with them." She placed the plates on a small table underneath a stained-glass window. "Her memory comes and goes. Most days she thinks she's Betsy Ross. So far she's stitched about eighty-five stars on a flag she's making." Amanda chuckled. "Poor old soul. It's sad to see a good mind go, but she seems happy."

Tanner brought the silver to the table. "I'm glad you bought her house. I've always liked this house."

"So have I."

"Is that four-poster bed still upstairs?"

He was standing so close, she could see the throbbing of his pulse in his throat. Memories and desire washed over her. She clutched the side of the table, hoping it would keep her from grabbing him and never letting go.

"Yes," she whispered.

When he reached out and put his hand on her shoulder, she thought she'd melt. Instead she stood perfectly motionless, hoping that starvation would keep her from doing something foolish.

"You were wearing green, just as you are now." His wonderful fingers massaged her through the silk of her blouse. "Remember, Mandy?"

"I don't want to remember."

"I think you do." He caught her other shoulder and turned her slowly toward him. With his forefingers he began tracing a slow line toward her breasts. The heat of his touch coursed through her. She saw the languid look of desire in his eyes as his fingertips found their mark. Her nipples were pointed and ready for more of his touch.

"It was in January."

"February." She considered it a miracle that she could talk. His hands were working magic, and she was completely under their spell. She could tell by his smile that he knew.

"It was so cold, we had three quilts on the bed."

"Four."

"You were wearing my ring. Remember, Mandy?"

She couldn't talk; she could barely breathe. But with Tanner's hands on her, she remembered. Oh, how she remembered. They had been newly engaged, full of plans for the future, and very much in love. They'd been house-sitting for Aunt Emma.

"I'll never forget the way you looked on that bed"—Tanner slowly popped open the top button of her blouse—"with your hair tumbled across the pillows." He undid the second button and slowly folded the silk aside. "And your eyes, enormous and shining in the moonlight . . ." His hand moved inside to caress her soft skin. "Remember how good it was, Mandy?" He bent down, nudging aside her bra and wetting her nipples with his tongue.

"Oh, yes." Her head lolled back, and she offered her breasts to him. She was so hungry, hungry for Tanner Donovan.

"I want you, Amanda. "

His voice was muffled against her skin. She tangled her hand in his dark hair, holding him there, wanting him so fiercely that she thought denial would kill her.

"Tanner." The word was a shattered plea. She felt an aching sense of loss when he left her breast, when he lifted his head and looked down at her.

"Amanda?"

"I'm . . ." She closed her eyes. There was no way she could regain her composure if she continued staring at him. She wet her dry lips with her tongue. "I'm hungry," she finally whispered.

With her eyes still closed, she felt his hands on her face, exploring, caressing, remembering.

"So am I. For you."

"Oh, please, Tanner. Don't."

She could feel the tension in his body as he held on to her, his hands moving down the side of her neck, over her shoulders, and down her arms. Opening her eyes, she saw that his struggle for control was as great as her own. She almost changed her mind. She almost yielded to him, fully aware that their loving would be no more to him than banishing old ghosts.

The silence stretched between them. It shouted to them, willing them to recall days gone by, times when they had spent love as freely and carelessly as rich Texans.

But there was no going back. Both of them knew it. The knowledge weighted down their hearts.

Tanner released her. "Food's getting cold."

"Yes." Amanda clenched her fists to still her shaking hands.

Tanner pulled out her chair, and she sat down. "Thank you."

"Just my natural good Southern manners."

"Not for the chair, for letting me go."

"Don't assign any lofty motives to me. I fully intend to bed you. But first I'm going to build up your endurance. Eleven years of deprivation won't be assuaged in a couple of hours."

The tenderness in his face belied his callous words. She had to look away from him to keep from reading into his look things she knew weren't there—love, and desire for a commitment. After fastening her bra and rebuttoning her blouse, she lifted the container full of Anna's chicken and dumplings from the picnic basket and filled their plates. She could feel Tanner's gaze on her, watching every move.

She wished she could wave a wand over them and wipe out the past. She wished there were magic words that would make starting over possible, but there was too much between them—loss of faith, loss of confidence. Most of all there was Claude. Whatever she and Tanner felt in each other's arms, she could never change the fact that she'd jilted him and married his best friend. She could hardly blame the man for wanting revenge. And yet she'd felt betrayed too. She never would have turned to another man if she hadn't felt that Tanner had placed a career and a chance at fame ahead of their relationship.

It was best, she decided, to get through the holidays with courage and all the savoir faire she could muster. After he was gone, then maybe she could put him out of her mind. Forever.

"These dumplings are delicious, Tanner."

"Mom will be pleased."

"You're very kind to bring them over."

"It was the least I could do after taking you on a picnic and feeding you only candy."

She laughed. "I believe you and I are doing a pretty good job of carrying on an ordinary conversation."

"I can be as ordinary as the next guy when I try. I can be as boring as hell."

"I never remember you as boring, Tanner."

"How do you remember me, Mandy?"

"Vital, aggressive, passionate—and totally committed to football."

Tanner decided to let her last comment slide. It didn't matter what she thought of him—then or now. Nothing mattered except putting her out of his life. Forever. Thirty-three was too damned old to be hurt all over again by Amanda Lassiter. Even if she did look like a saint and kiss like a sinner. Lord, that mouth. He'd give up his fortune for the right to taste her lips every day.

He realized too late that he should have stayed home with his dumplings. He was treading on dangerous ground, being in this house with her and all their memories. It was going to take every ounce of his willpower to get through the evening without falling in love with her again.

He decided his best defense would be a good offense. He hated what he had to do but believed he could never risk loving and losing her again. *Forgive me, Amanda. It's the only way.*

"You're a beautiful woman, Amanda."

"Thank you."

Her trusting smile didn't make it any easier for him. "How is it that you never used your looks to lead another man to the altar after Claude?"

At the sudden intake of her breath and the flashing of anger in her eyes, he felt regret and guilt. Her smile was so much more pleasurable. He could bask in it for a hundred years and never tire of it. With effort he remembered her betrayal.

"That *is* the way you came between me and my best friend, isn't it, Mandy?"

She stood slowly, using her body as a weapon. With languorous movements she laced her hands behind her neck and lifted her glorious hair upward. She arched her body so that her perfect breasts were thrust forward.

"Yes." Her voice was low, sultry, sexy. Only the high spots of color on her cheeks and her blazing eyes betrayed her anger.

She lowered her arms, letting her hair drift through her fingers. "Like this, Tanner."

Her eyes never left his as she unbuttoned her blouse again. He could almost hear the silk against her skin as she caressed the material, dragging it inch by sensuous inch off her shoulders.

"I made him want me, Tanner." Her hands were on the waistband of her slacks. "I used my body."

The zipper was loud, like sandpaper grating on his frayed nerves. She hooked her thumbs into her waistband and lowered the slacks. The black lace she wore teased, provoked. His breathing became harsh. With maddening slowness her hips came into view, alluring, curving away from her tiny waist, just the way he remembered. She stepped out of the slacks, kicking them out of her way.

Her legs were gorgeous, their length and shape emphasized by the black lace teddy with French-cut sides. She put her hands on her hips. "Claude wanted my body, Tanner. Do you?"

He wanted it so badly, he thought he'd go mad.

"In my own time, Amanda."

She wasn't finished with her revenge. Leaning down, she stroked him, taking her time, letting him know the full electricity of her touch. Then she straightened, her expression cool and detached. Letting her left hand slide across her shoulder and down her arm, she lowered one strap of her black teddy. Her right breast, mere inches from his mouth, tantalized him.

"Feast your eyes, Tanner, for you'll never be able to do more than look again. You had your time eleven years ago."

With magnificent control she walked away from him. Turning in the doorway, she sank one last barb. "Just remember, I chose Claude."

He could hear her progress through the house. Each door she slammed punctuated the restless silence. Her footsteps on the stairs clapped with the finality of doom. He sat at the table, wondering at the havoc he had wrought. Guilt slashed through him. In his zeal to protect himself he'd wounded Amanda. Revenge was bitter, and catharsis didn't matter anymore. What mattered was that he had driven away the only woman he had ever loved, the only woman he *could* ever love. Too late, the realization swept over him. Heaven help him, he was in love with Amanda once more. Probably had been from the day he saw her walk into Jimmy's. What had happened eleven years ago was over and done with. Finished. He could forgive the past, but he could never forgive himself if he lost Amanda again.

He'd been fooling himself. All his notions about bedding and forgetting her had been a sham. It was ironic to him that he could be so clearheaded in business and so blind about love. His heart had been shouting the truth to him ever since he'd come home, but he had refused to listen. He'd plunged stubbornly ahead, widening the chasm that was already between them. Winning her again would have been difficult at best; now he had made it almost impossible.

A lesser man might have given up, but Tanner Donovan was a stranger to defeat. With the wonderful knowledge of love coursing through him like new wine, he never considered any possibility except winning. He would have her, and any man who tried to come between them had better be prepared to do battle with the devil.

First he smiled, then the smile became a chuckle, and the chuckle became a full-bodied roar of sheer joy. Amanda would lead him a merry chase, but he'd have her. This time for keeps.

He went to the kitchen door and listened. There was no sound from Amanda. Knowing her, he decided that she was probably hatching a plan that would make tonight's skirmish seen tame.

He smiled. "Brava, Amanda. You're a hell of a lady."

Clearing the table, he stored the leftovers in the refrigerator, then searched the cabinets until he'd found a pencil and notepaper. His handwriting was as bold as he was. "This time, Amanda, you'll choose me."

He propped the note on the table, picked up his picnic basket, and headed through the house. The next day he would begin the romance of the century. Tonight he needed to make plans.

Upstairs, Amanda heard the whistling. She stopped her restless pacing to listen. It didn't surprise her that the man who'd received a crushing blow at her hands should be whistling. That was Tanner, through and through. Arrogant to a fault, self-confident to the core. In spite of her turmoil, she smiled. Any other man would be down there licking his wounds, and Tanner Donovan was whistling. It wasn't a funeral dirge, either. The song was "Get Me to the Church on Time." She knew the lyrics well, for she'd played the role of Eliza Doolittle her freshman year at the University of Southern Mississippi. Weekends, when she was visiting him in Alabama, Tanner had cued her. Quick study that he was, he'd learned all the songs also.

"What is that rake up to now?" She went to her bedroom door, half expecting him to come storming up the stairs. Instead she heard the front door slam.

"So, I've sent him home in defeat." But she knew, even as she said the words, that it wasn't true. Tanner was never defeated and rarely retreated. She was glad. In spite of the blood she'd drawn, she had no desire to hurt him. She was merely defending herself, covering her vulnerability with bravado.

She hurried to her bedroom window and drew back the curtain. Tanner was getting into his car.

She supposed it was instinct that made him know he was being watched. He looked up. The smile he gave her had enough voltage to light every Christmas tree in Greenville. She almost forgot their encounter in the kitchen.

He stood in the moonlight, bold and impossibly handsome, a real hero, and not just according to the papers, she thought. He was a man who had succeeded at everything he'd attempted, a generous man who had used his wealth and fame to endow libraries and build orphanages and establish scholarships. And a dangerously charming man who thumbed his nose at failure and whistled in the face of defeat.

She pressed her forehead against the windowpane. "Oh, Lord, Tanner. I *won't* fall in love with you again."

It was almost as if he had heard her.

"Amanda!" he called.

Every fiber of common sense she possessed warned her to ignore him. Instead she opened the window.

"Go away, Tanner. It's over between us."

"It will never be over between us. Remember that, Amanda." He blew her a kiss, climbed into his flashy car, and drove off.

Amanda made herself turn away from the window and not watch his car disappear down the street. She would have an ordinary evening, she vowed. She'd address Christmas cards and call Aunt Emma, and maybe even bake a cake.

She went to the small cherry-wood desk in her bedroom and took out her cards. With great determination she sat down and picked up her pen. An enormous restlessness continued to stir in her. Maybe she should bake the cake first.

She started toward the kitchen, then remembered her paltry supply of staples. There was not enough flour to make a cupcake, let alone a whole cake, and she had less than a quart of milk and no sugar.

She prowled and paced through her house half a dozen times, then suddenly remembered that the drive-in theater ran all-night movies on Mondays. Even during the winter.

Amanda loved the movies, and she wasn't discriminating—horror, fantasy, drama, classics, musicals—it didn't matter what was showing. She enjoyed immersing herself in the make-believe world of the movies.

She got her coat from the hall closet and was headed out the door when the phone rang. She picked it up.

"Hello, darling. It's your Aunt Barbara."

Amanda sighed. The only thing more long-winded than Aunt Barbara was a freight train full of hot-air balloons.

"Hello, Aunt Barbara. How are you?"

Aunt Barbara began to tell her, in minute detail, exactly how she was. Amanda resigned herself to missing the first two shows at the drive-in.

Tanner whistled all the way home. He was still whistling when he bounded up the steps to his house.

"Tanner's home," he heard his dad say. "Nobody bangs the front door the way he does."

He walked down the hall and stuck his head around the door. His parents were sitting in front of the fire. "Hi, Mom, Pop. Is that popcorn I smell?"

Matthew Donovan laughed. "What did I tell you, Anna? That boy can smell popcorn a mile away. I might as well make another popper full."

Tanner held up his hand. "None for me. I have things to do. Have fun, you two. See you later." He left, whistling.

With visions of Amanda dancing in his head, he went upstairs and made his calls. When he had finished, he gave a satisfied chuckle. He had set the wheels of romance turning, and now all he had to do was be patient—a completely new role for him.

He picked up a magazine and flipped through it. Nothing *Newsweek* had to say interested him. He stuck a tape into the player, but that was a mistake. It was a love song, and it reminded him of Amanda. He turned it off. In his state of mind he'd be likely to storm her house and take her by force. That wouldn't do. Not at all. He had to court and woo and romance her again. Starting tomorrow.

Grabbing his jacket, he headed down the stairs. There was one place he could go when he needed to forget everything and make time pass quickly— the movies. Picking up the newspaper from the hall table, he searched for the entertainment section. To his delight the drive-in still had all-night movies on Mondays. Tonight's fare was horror— *The Creature of Darkness, Witches of Lust, Black Lagoon, Over My Dead Body,* and *Girl of My Nightmares.* He laughed. That last one sounded intriguing.

The drive-in theater was practically deserted. He parked near the concession stand, bought himself the largest tub of buttered popcorn, three hot dogs, a cup of hot chocolate, and two Hershey bars with almonds, and settled in for a movie marathon.

The first movie was already half over, but that didn't matter. Tanner had the whole thing figured out in five minutes. The good guys would save the town from the creature.

They finally did, just as Amanda's car drove by. Tanner craned his neck to follow her progress.

Apparently she didn't see him, for she never looked in his direction. Her car cruised down the lane and eased into a slot two rows in front of his. There was nothing to mar his view of her except two speaker posts. He felt his heart quicken. Sentimental fool, he thought, chiding himself. He leaned forward to get a better view. Her hair glowed in the fluorescent lights. He'd never realized how sexy the back of a woman's head could be. He gazed at her, imagining the feel of that hair against his cheek.

The squawking of his speaker box made him jump. To his chagrin he realized his hand was buried in the tub of buttered popcorn and had been since Amanda had driven by. Furthermore he had no idea how the movie had ended.

He wiped the butter off and considered joining her. Then he had second thoughts. Like him, she'd always used movies as a means of escape. She probably needed this evening of privacy as much as he did. Strange, he thought, how loving a person could make a difference. Yesterday he would have gotten boldly into her car, pulled her into his arms, and taken what he wanted. Tonight he couldn't be that selfish. He would never again touch her without consideration of her feelings. The next time he kissed her, she'd know it was love.

Tanner leaned back to watch the second movie, *Witches of Lust*. Just his luck, one of the beauties on the screen looked too much like Amanda for his comfort. When the movie progressed from the witch part to the lust part, Tanner had to clench his fists to keep from leaping out of his car and getting into Amanda's. The times he and Amanda had petted at the drive-in movies! he thought agonizingly. His windows were steamed up simply from thinking about it.

He reached for a cold hot dog and tried to concentrate on the movie.

Amanda fidgeted in her car. The movie would have helped her forget, she decided, if it weren't so sensuous. Probably what she needed was a big box of buttered popcorn. It would be hard to eat, watch, and think at the same time.

She hung her speaker back on the pole and got out of her car. There was Tanner, as big as life, sitting two rows back in his red Corvette, leaning back and grinning at her. No, leering. That's what he was doing. She felt her silly heart bump against her rib cage.

I'll ignore him, she vowed.

She turned around and marched straight ahead to the concession stand, never looking in his direction. On the return trip, her buttered popcorn clutched in her hands, she tried to discipline herself to ignore him still. But she couldn't. She felt compelled to glance in his direction. He lifted his hand in salute. She gave a slight nod, as if seeing him didn't bother her at all, and then she climbed into her car. She was concentrating so hard on appearing unruffled that she tangled her foot in the speaker cord. The speaker squawked as it bit the dust. Using all the dignity she could muster, she rescued it, got into her car, and hung the devilish contraption on the side of her door.

She stared straight ahead, looking at the screen without seeing a thing and eating her popcorn without tasting a bite. Oh, Lord, she thought, the times she and Tanner had loved at the drive-in!

There had been other times, too, fun times with a gang of kids from the high school. Carefree times when Claude had stolen the show by telling them all some outrageous story that made the movie pale by comparison. Claude, she thought. He was between them like a wall. She wondered if Tanner was thinking of him too.

She could feel Tanner back there. She could picture the ways his quicksilver eyes gleamed with the flashy drive-in lights shining in them. It made her feel hollow to look straight ahead and pretend she didn't notice him, to pretend she didn't care.

The movie finally ended. Her neck was stiff. As the reels were being changed, she rubbed the back of neck, tilting her head this way and that to loosen the muscles. It seemed only natural that she should glance back at Tanner. Just a glance, she told herself.

He was looking at her. Even from two rows back she could tell. She saw him smile. She ached to touch him. The need was so strong that she felt foolish sitting in her car denying herself.

Following her impulse, she opened her door and started walking his way. She'd say hello, a casual greeting between two adults. All the way to his car she rationalized her motives.

She could feel the heat of his glance as he watched her walk. Breathing deeply, she tried to slow the trip-hammer rhythm of her heart. It was useless. By the time she leaned toward his window, she felt as if she'd run a twenty-six-mile marathon.

She rested her hand on the door. "Hello, Tanner."

"Amanda!"

She wished his eyes wouldn't gleam so. It made being casual very hard.

"Enjoying the movies?" Brilliant, she thought, chiding herself. Nor only did she sound breathless, she sounded simpleminded.

"Yes. Are you?"

His smile was so endearing, she almost didn't notice that he seemed as ill at ease as she.

"Yes." She knew there were other words in her vocabulary, but she couldn't think of them. She figured she'd think of all sorts of witty replies as soon as she got back in her car.

Tanner put his hand over hers. "Won't you join me? There's room for two."

"No." The word hung in the air as they looked at each other. There'd always been a form of telepathy between them, messages they relayed with their eyes. She knew he wanted her. The naked desire was there, gleaming in his eyes. She wondered if she'd masked her own desire.

"You'll get cold standing out there."

His voice was like a caress, his tone gentle with concern. The sound of it made her feel warm and protected and cherished. With great clarity she saw how easy it would be to love him again. She knew she should go, but she wanted to feel his hand on hers a moment longer.

"No," she said. "I won't be standing here that long."

"I see."

He flashed that endearing smile again, and still she couldn't go.

"Please thank Anna for the chicken and dumplings."

"I will."

Even though the night had turned cooler, she felt warm through and through. She thought it was remarkable that Tanner could do that to her simply by touching her hand—and after all these years.

She leaned closer. "I'll call on her soon and thank her in person."

"She'll like that."

His face was so close, she could see a tiny smear of butter on his cheek.

"You have butter."

"Where?" His gaze never left hers.

"There." She lifted her free hand and touched the spot on his cheek. Such a simple touch, and yet she felt as if she'd been plugged into the socket with the Christmas-tree lights.

"Thank you."

"You're welcome." Reluctantly she removed her hand. "It's time to go. Good-bye, Tanner."

She was two steps away when he called her name.

"Amanda . . ."

Joy leapt in her as she turned back around.

"I have something for you."

As she stepped back to his car all sorts of thoughts ran through her mind. He'd lean out the window and kiss her; he'd pull her through the window and hold her; he'd get out and carry her into the concession stand, draped across his shoulder like a sack of potatoes, and make love to her right there under the fluorescent lights, where he'd have a big audience.

He did none of those things. Instead he held out a candy bar.

"Your favorite. I bought two so we could share."

"How did you know I was coming?"

"I didn't. I guess I just secretly hoped you would."

"That's sweet, Tanner. Thank you."

"You're welcome."

"Well . . . good-bye again."

"Good-bye."

As she walked back to her car she pondered on what had happened, how polite they'd been. They'd acted like two strangers trying to make a good impression. It was all very puzzling to her—and best not to analyze.

She climbed into her car, adjusted her speaker, and leaned back to watch the last movie. She hoped to fall into oblivion. All she felt was nervous anticipation and a tingling in her spine.

But she was determined not to leave. Then Tanner would know. What he would know, she couldn't say, nor did she want to consider it.

Tanner's breathing didn't get back to normal

until Amanda was back in her car. Reaching for a Hershey bar, he tried to pretend she wasn't up there in her car, tempting him beyond endurance, but he knew it was useless. Every minute that crawled by seemed to whisper her name.

He was determined to stay. Having her where he could see her for the next two hours was a gift too precious to throw away, even if he did have to suffer.

When the last show had ended, Tanner and Amanda started their cars and drove slowly down the dirt lanes between the speaker posts. They held a parallel course until they came to the exit. Then Amanda's car turned in one direction, and Tanner's in the other.

They went their separate ways.

Tuesday morning, Amanda was awakened by the doorbell. She pulled the covers over her head and mumbled, half asleep, "Go away."

The persistent ringing jolted her out of bed. Picking up her terry-cloth robe and raking her hand through her tangled hair, she started down the stairs. By the time she was at the front door, she was fully awake.

"Special delivery for Miss Amanda Lassiter."

The delivery boy was hidden behind a bouquet of orchids.

"I'm Amanda Lassiter."

"Would you sign here, ma'am?" He held out a clipboard and a pen. As she wrote, he talked. "Never seen the likes of it. This dude calls up Miss Chotley—that's the owner of the shop, you know, Miss Chotley—calls her up in the middle of the night and orders these Hawaiian flowers. These ain't your regular hothouse variety, see. These here are the exotic kind. Don't grow 'em nowhere 'cept the Islands." He laughed. "That's how we in the business refer to Hawaii—the Islands. Anyhow, Miss Chotley says she don't have 'em in stock, and this dude says to have 'em shipped in. He'll pay. He insisted it had to be done last night too. Wanted you to have 'em first thing this morning. He must be rich as Grease Us, or whatever that storybook feller's name is."

Amanda had to smile. Only one man would make such a production of sending a bouquet. Any other man would have been satisfied with roses, but not Tanner. As she took the flowers she saw his bold signature on the card and thought how he would have enjoyed the delivery boy's monologue. Tanner had always loved the limelight; being a legend tickled his fancy.

Her smile changed to a grin of pure devilment.

"His name is Tanner Donovan, and he *is* rich as Croesus."

"I wondered if it wadn't him. I knew he was back in town. Comes home every Christmas, they say. That man sure was a giant on the football field."

"Generous too. I've heard he plans to send flowers to every available woman over thirty in Greenville."

"Golly, Miss Lassiter." She watched the boy's eyes widen. "Won't that cost him a bundle?"

"Probably so, but Tanner Donovan has sworn to give every one of us a thrill. Can you imagine the Christmas joy he'll spread with his wonderful flowers?"

"Not to mention that Miss Chotley will make a killing out of the deal. Golly!"

Amanda gave him a generous tip and sent him on his way. Her conscience barely twinged over what she had done and what she was about to do. What woman wouldn't love to get a long-stemmed red rose at Christmastime, she rationalized. Especially from Tanner Donovan. He did so love the limelight! The prank would cost her, but one-upmanship was never cheap. She owed him for the abduction in the surrey, not to mention the scene at the country club.

She made her list, then picked up the phone and called the florist.

Tanner whistled around his house all morning. Matthew finally told him he was disturbing every hound dog between Greenville and Columbus, and Anna, who knew about the dumplings, smiled a secret smile.

He wondered if Amanda had found his note in the kitchen, if she had received the orchids, and what she would do when she did.

He wasn't long in finding out.

At ten o'clock the phone rang. It was Miss Amy Glenn Hughes, calling to thank Tanner for the long-stemmed red rose. He was sure there had been a mistake, but he decided to play along and see what he could find out.

"You got the rose?"

"Oh, yes. This morning." Amy Hughes's cooing reminded him of the pigeons in the barn's loft. "And the note too."

"I was always good with words." He figured that for once his immodesty would serve him well. "Would you read it to me? I'd like to know if it sounds as good now as it did when I wrote it."

"What a pistol you are!" He could hear Amy Hughes twittering and fluttering like a wren at a bluebird party as she scratched around for the note. "Here it is, Tanner: 'If I can do anything to make your holidays brighter, let me know.' Signed by you." Amy Hughes sighed. "What a lovely surprise."

Only Amanda would think of such a clever way to pay him back and at the same time do a good deed, he decided. No purpose would be served in telling Amy Hughes that he hadn't sent the rose. "Can I do anything to make your holidays brighter?"

"You already have. Thank you so much for the flower."

"You are very welcome. Have a wonderful Christmas."

"You too."

Amy Hughes's call was the first of fifteen he received that morning—all thanking him for the long-stemmed red rose. He was so busy answering the telephone that he had no time to think about romance. But he *did* think about Amanda. Between calls he grinned and chuckled and slapped his thigh and talked to himself until Theo's oldest boy walked by and asked him what in the world ailed him.

"Love," Tanner said.

"I hope it's not catching. It's making you weird, Uncle Tanner."

"Your time will come."

Kenneth said a forbidden word and loped up the stairs.

Tanner chuckled and mentally calculated how old he would be when he and Amanda had teenage sons. Not too old to enjoy them if they started right away, he decided. Time was wasting.

He got into his car and headed to the most exclusive jewelry store in Greenville.

The package was delivered to Amanda's shop that same afternoon.

The emerald-and-diamond necklace caught the sun and reflected rainbows on her walls. Even as she reached for the card she knew who had sent it. "If there's anything I can do to make your holidays brighter, let me know," the card said. "P.S. Let's see you duplicate this with fifteen of Greenville's lonesome ladies."

Maxine leaned over her shoulder and gasped. "What a stunning piece of jewelry. Tanner sent it?"

"Yes." Amanda held it to the light, turning it this way and that, imagining how it would look in the open neck of her ivory silk dress. She loved flamboyant jewelry, always had. Her jewelry box at home was stuffed with the antique pieces she'd bought for her shop over the years and couldn't bear to part with. Nothing she had would compare with this necklace, though. The piece was exquisite—and very expensive. Reluctantly she put the necklace in the box and closed the lid. "Not that it matters. I can't keep it."

"For Pete's sake, why not? The man's crazy about you. And he certainly can afford it. That's a mere bauble to him."

"Nonetheless, I'm taking it back to him."

"Why?"

"The flowers were just a game. Jewelry is serious business."

"Flowers? What flowers?"

"Tanner sent orchids this morning."

"Amanda, that man is a sweetheart. Grab him while you can."

"That man is nothing but trouble. The necklace goes back as soon as I close the shop. That's final." She carried the box to her safe.

"You probably don't believe in Santa Claus, either."

Amanda laughed. "Don't look so crestfallen, Maxine. I believe in Santa Claus; I just don't believe in Tanner Donovan."

She didn't believe in Tanner, she told herself later that afternoon as she left her shop and drove straight to his house. He was as unpredictable as the wind. Today he was spending time with her, but only because it amused him. Who knew what would hold his interest the next day? All the Donovans had a wild streak. He might decide to buy a rugby team and traipse off to England or to Australia. Even if she did have feelings for the man, she wasn't about to settle for leftover love and part-time attention. It hadn't been enough before, and it wasn't enough now.

As she parked her Honda in front of the Donovans' sprawling Victorian house, she noticed that Tanner's car was not in sight. She could almost taste her disappointment. All during her drive into the country she had pictured exactly how he would look when he came to the door, the endearing way his dark hair would be tousled across his forehead, the exact gleam of mischief and pleasure in his quicksilver eyes, the way he would walk, with that bold, casual grace that only an athlete possessed.

Anna Donovan opened the door. Amanda rarely saw her, except from up in the choir loft on Sundays. She had forgotten how dear Anna always looked, standing in her doorway, smiling that warm welcome.

"Hello, Anna."

Anna held out her arms. "Amanda! It's so good to have you here again."

Anna had always been gracious and charming, even after she'd jilted Tanner, Amanda thought as she returned the hug.

"Let me look at you. My, my. As pretty as a picture. Won't Tanner be glad to see you!"

Probably not, Amanda thought, but she didn't tell Anna so.

"Thank you for the chicken and dumplings, Anna. They were delicious."

"You're so welcome, dear. Tanner's always been so thoughtful, even when he was a little boy. He used to go out in the pasture and pick me a bouquet, just because he liked to see me smile, he'd say. I never had the heart to tell him he was picking bitter weeds. Listen to me going on about Tanner and letting you stand out in the cold." She took Amanda's arm and led her into the house. "Come in, my dear, and warm your feet by the fire. Theo's boys built a big one in the library." She chatted on as she showed Amanda into the cozy, book-lined room she called the library. "All the menfolk have gone off to get a Christmas tree. We're expecting Paul and his family tomorrow. We always wait for the twins to come before we trim the tree. Little Matthew is the spitting image of Paul. Did you know Martie's expecting again?"

"No. That's lovely." Amanda felt a strange twinge of envy and regret. She'd wanted children. Claude had too. After three years of trying, they'd finally sought professional help. Claude had been sterile. She'd mourned her unborn children as if they'd had names and faces. The lack of children, as much as anything, had contributed to the breakup of their marriage.

If she and Tanner had married, would they have had a family by now? Would one of them have been a miniature Tanner? She felt empty, and for the first time in her life she felt old. Thirty-three and no children. No one to help trim a tree, no one to play Santa for, no little hands to hold, no sweet heads to tousle.

She firmly pushed the thoughts away and turned her attention back to her hostess. Anna was asking about her parents.

"They're fine. They're spending Christmas in England."

"They always did love to travel." Anna's face suddenly lit up. "I do believe I hear the men."

Amanda did too. Something inside her leapt at the sound of Tanner's voice. She folded her hands in her lap and tried to look serene.

The Donovan men came through the door—Matthew, Charles, Glover, Theo, and Tanner. Only Paul and Jacob were missing. They were all tall, rugged, handsome men, even Matthew with his shock of gray hair. They were laughing and joking as Matthew directed Theo and Tanner, carrying an enormous tree, through the library door.

The tree blocked Amanda from view, so she got to watch them unobserved. She treasured the family scene, cherished it, stored it in her memory to recall in the lonesome times after Christmas when Tanner would be back in Dallas and she would be alone.

"It's crooked," Theo said.

"It has dignity," Tanner said.

"You say that because you picked it out," Charles said.

Anna stood and clapped her hands. "My, my, it's a lovely tree, boys, but do say hello to our guest."

The Donovan men turned to Amanda. They smiled and greeted her, all at once. Except Tanner, and she had eyes only for him. He leaned casually against the mantel, looking at her as if he planned to cover her with whipped cream and have her for dessert.

She didn't know what she said to the Donovan men. Years of training in small talk had carried her through, for her gaze was locked with Tanner's. She saw the tiny flames ignite in their depths, noted the languid drooping of his lids. The desire to love and to be loved by this man had never been stronger. And she thanked her lucky stars that the room was full of people.

"I have a big pot of coffee in the kitchen," Anna said. "I can serve it in here, or perhaps you'd like to come back there. A fresh pan of gingerbread ought to be ready in about ten minutes."

"Amanda and I will join you in the kitchen later." It was the first time Tanner had spoken. Amanda didn't miss the significant glances the Donovan men gave each other as they filed out behind Anna. Matthew discreetly closed the door.

"I've been wanting to kiss you since I walked into this room and saw you sitting over there." In three steps he was beside her. He pulled her into his arms and held her tight. "Lord, you feel good."

"Tanner." She knew she'd made only a token protest. She could no more resist his arms than she could fly. He pressed her head against his shoulder. It fit perfectly—as it always had.

"It's been almost twenty-four hours since I've seen you, Mandy. I don't intend to let that happen again." He tipped her head back with one finger. "You're so damned beautiful, I ache every time I look at you."

Then his lips were on hers. He tasted of wind and pine trees and soap. It was the tenderest of kisses, a warm, sweet sensation that enfolded her heart. There was no urgency, no demand in the kiss, only a precious touching. If she hadn't known better, she would have thought it was the kiss of a man in love. Fortunately she did know better. It made what she had to do much easier.

The sweetness continued for so long, her resolve faltered. She was caught up in the embrace. The crackling hearth fire warmed her outside, and the delicious heat of Tanner's kiss warmed her inside. As they kissed, his hands gently massaged her back, tenderly smoothed her hair. She died a little inside, knowing it couldn't last forever.

Finally Tanner drew back, but he kept his hold on her, cupping her face and holding it so close to his that they seemed to breathe as one.

"I love you, Mandy."

He said it simply; she almost believed him. But

her good common sense told her it was merely his latest ploy.

"Once I believed that. Not anymore, Tanner."

Silently Tanner cursed the fates that had torn them apart and set them on separate paths. Inside, he raged against the empty years and her marriage to Claude. He even raged against the football career that had been the beginning of the end for them.

He wanted to smash his fist against the wall. He wanted to run until he fell in his tracks. He wanted to shout his fury until the very rafters of the house fell down. Instead, he continued holding her beautiful face, his thumbs massaging her jaw as he gazed down at her.

"I'll make you believe it."

Letting her go, knowing she didn't believe in his love, was one of the hardest things he'd ever done. He released her, realizing that winning her again would take time. At that moment he wished for some of the superpowers the press had credited him with when he was quarterbacking for the Texas Titans. Since he had none, he'd have to rely on instinct to get him through the game, the most important game of all. He'd call the plays as he saw them. Serious, playful, passionate—he'd be whatever it took to win Amanda again.

Her laugh was shaky. The sound of it made him sad and happy at the same time; he felt sad because he was the cause, and happy because her unease gave him hope.

He watched as she sat down in the chair, smoothed her skirt over her knees, tossed her head in defiance.

"Never. Your expectations are exceeded only by your arrogance."

Thank God, he thought, she had gotten her spunkiness back.

"I take that as a challenge, Mandy. And you know how I love a challenge."

"Almost as much as you love being outrageous." She dug into her purse and held up the jewelry box. "I believe this belongs to you."

"No. It belongs to you."

"I can't accept diamonds and emeralds from you. Give them to somebody else."

He took the box and unsnapped the lid. "These are yours, and you will have them." He undid the clasp. "Don't pull away, Amanda. I've waited all day to see them against your skin." He leaned down to fasten them at her throat.

She pushed his hands aside. "Then you bought them for your own amusement?"

"For amusement, for love. Take your choice."

"Amusement, then. But be forewarned, Tanner. I don't plan to be your plaything. You'll have to amuse yourself with someone else."

His laugh was one of pure delight. "You amuse me, Mandy, whether you want to or not. You delight me; you enchant me. And I'm going to enjoy romancing you every bit as much as I enjoyed trying to maneuver you into my bed."

"Aren't they one and the same, Tanner?"

"You know damned well they're not. You can't pretend brittleness with me and get by with it. I know you too well."

"And I know you too well to fall under your spell a second time. The surrey didn't work; the flowers didn't work. And neither will the necklace. Tanner, you're a gorgeous man, a mouth-wateringly handsome man. . . ."

"That's a nice start."

"I don't deny that I feel desire in your arms. . . ."

"I'll accept that too."

"But I can never trust your love again."

"You can and you will." He scooped her from

the chair and held her fiercely to him. The necklace, still dangling from his hand, bit into her flesh. Tanner had her so mesmerized, she hardly noticed.

"Stubborn woman. I could kiss you into submission."

"Is this your notion of romance? Caveman tactics went out years ago."

Tanner hoped the flush on her cheeks and the brightness in her eyes meant that he was disturbing her. He knew the passions that raged beneath her cool exterior. With effort he held himself in check. Romance, not mere sex, was the object here. He was looking for a lifetime commitment, not quick relief.

"Texas Titans have a lot to learn. Teach me, Amanda."

She chuckled. "Do you know how hard you are to resist when you get that little-boy-waiting-for-Christmas look on your face? You must practice that look in the mirror."

"I learned it from Paul. He always used it to wheedle the biggest piece of gingerbread out of Mom. It took me three years to catch on."

"Speaking of gingerbread, I'm hungry. Didn't Anna mention that she had a fresh batch in the oven?"

"Have you had dinner, Mandy?"

"No. I came straight from the shop."

"I'll bet you never even had breakfast."

"I was too busy doing other things."

He laughed. "Ordering roses?"

"Yes. Maxine saved my life this morning by bringing in a couple of doughnuts."

"Good lord, woman! You're going to die of malnutrition before I can get you to the altar." Keeping her firmly against him, he set her on her feet. "Madame, I am taking you to Doe's for dinner." In one swift movement he had the necklace fastened around her neck.

"What are you doing?"

"I like my woman to wear diamonds and emeralds."

"I'm not your woman, and I'm not keeping them."

"Humor me."

"Only for tonight, until just after I've had the steak as big as a suitcase and the potatoes with sour cream and a salad as big as Lake Ferguson. Then I'll have six Hershey bars with almonds."

His hearty roar of laughter nearly toppled the crooked Christmas tree. "I thought food was the way to a *man's* heart."

"Somebody got their sexes mixed, obviously."

Taking her by the hand, he led her through the house and out to his car. They laughed all the way.

Six

They still were laughing when Tanner parked beside an insignificant-looking old storefront, tucked out of sight on Nelson Street. If he hadn't known the restaurant so well, he might have missed it. The sign, Doe's Eat Place, was illuminated by one dim bulb. There was no glitz, no ostentation, only good food that drew local customers like sinners to a tent revival, and even brought in the hungry hordes from Tupelo and Memphis and Birmingham.

"There's a big crowd tonight, Mandy. I do love a large audience."

"One of the things I've always liked about you is that you never pretend to be someone you're not. It gladdens my heart to see that you're the same egotistical man I jilted."

He pretended to be crestfallen. "Mandy, how you wound me."

"I can tell by the twinkle in your eye that you're crushed to the bone. It'll take you at least two seconds to recover."

"The only thing that will make me recover is for you to wear these." He reached into his pockets and pulled out a pair of emerald-and-diamond earrings, mates to the necklace she was wearing.

"Do you always carry a fortune in jewels in your pocket?"

"Only since I came back to Greenville and saw you again. You've enchanted me."

The look in his eyes belied his lighthearted words. A great confusion rose in Amanda. Rebuffing a Tanner who vowed to bed her and leave her had been difficult; refusing a Tanner who vowed he loved her was almost impossible. She didn't know what was true anymore. Once she and Tanner had loved so fiercely, they'd believed it could never end. But it had. Dare she take that chance again? Even if she risked loving and losing again, there was Claude. He stood between them, a reminder that she'd broken more than an engagement; she'd broken a friendship.

Amanda willed herself to ignore Tanner's mesmerizing charm.

"You'll get over it."

"I don't plan to."

With one arm he drew her across the seat toward him. He was so compellingly sensuous, so delicious he could substitute for that steak dinner.

Tanner's hand on her felt hot as he stroked her hair, outlined her jaw, traced the pattern of jewels against her throat. It took all her willpower to pretend aloofness.

"I love you in silk. You remind me of an angel."

"I'm not."

He chuckled. "How well I know. A fallen one, perhaps, but certainly no angel." Placing his forefinger on her lips, he traced them lightly. "Your lips bewitch me, Mandy. I can barely endure not kissing them."

"A latent attack of scruples?"

"No. If I start now, I won't be satisfied with

merely taking your mouth. I'll have to have it all."
He brushed his hands down her cheek, lingering
on the soft curve of her jaw. "And I intend to, but
not in Doe's parking lot."

She closed her eyes in relief. If he had made one
more move toward her, she wouldn't have been
able to say no.

"Dreaming?" Tanner teased.

"No. Counting my blessings."

"I hope you have one hundred, Mandy, and that
I'm ninety-nine of them."

She laughed in genuine appreciation of his lovable arrogance. "You *are* the same outrageous
man who could walk into a room and create a riot
among the women just by the way you stood."

"Are you ready to create a stir?"

"Haven't we always?"

"Yes. It wouldn't do to disappoint our friends
and neighbors." He fastened the diamonds and
emeralds on her ears, then leaned back to ap-
praise her. "Gorgeous, but it lacks something."
Reaching into his pocket, he pulled out a matching bracelet.

"Tanner, you're insane."

"No. I'm wealthy. Hold out your arm, Mandy."

"A bit flashy for Doe's, don't you think?"

"You're a woman who should be noticed."

"I think you've guaranteed that."

He brushed his lips lovingly against her cheek.
"No. God did that when he made you." The chill
wind whipped her hair as he opened the car door
and helped her out. Her jewelry caught the light
of the evening star and shot a thousand bright
prisms into the darkness.

Heads turned when they walked into Doe's, and
it wasn't caused by the jewelry. Tanner and
Amanda had been Greenville's golden couple, gorgeous, successful, two hometown favorites who

had seemed fated for one another. Whispers and stares followed them as they were escorted to a table. Speculation ran high among the locals who remembered their courtship, and the wedding where Tanner had tried to snatch her out of the arms of another man. Most of the women sighed and declared to their spouses that romance was ablossom again, and the men countered by saying that Tanner Donovan was merely amusing himself until he could go back to that robust Texas town where money flowed liked confessions at a river baptizing, and women were as plentiful as honeybees in a clover field—and twice as sweet.

"Every man in this room wants you." Tanner leaned across the table and took Amanda's hand. "I'm intensely jealous."

"You know how to play a role to the hilt. I remember how you used to ham it up when you helped me with all those college theatrical productions."

"You were very good, Amanda. Do you do any theater now?"

"Not since I left Fulton."

"Why did you leave Fulton—and Claude?"

"Tanner, don't. Not that again."

"I have to know, Amanda. Did you love him?"

"Why didn't you ask that question years ago, when I returned your ring?"

"Pride. Fear. Who knows? I'm asking now."

She took a deep breath. It was time to get this out in the open. In many ways Tanner deserved to know.

"A lot of things happened in our marriage, little irritations that multiplied and got out of hand. Underlying all the small problems was the big one; we couldn't have children. Claude was sterile." She'd saved the hardest part for last. Taking another deep breath, she continued. "I loved him, Tanner, but in the end it wasn't enough."

She was sorry for the quick flash of pain she saw in his eyes. A great urge to spare him welled up in her, but she instinctively knew that there had to be nothing but truth between them that night. She squeezed his hand. "I did, Tanner," she said quietly. "Claude was a good man, a steady, reliable, warmhearted man. And I loved him—but never the way I loved you."

He closed his eyes briefly, then captured her gaze with a look of such stunning intensity that she had to clench her teeth to keep from taking him into her arms and never letting go.

"Thank you for telling me that. As much as it hurts to know you loved another man, I don't think I could have forgiven your marrying my best friend for any reason except love."

"And have you forgiven me, Tanner?"

"Yes."

"I'm glad. Guilt is a heavy burden."

"Too heavy for your beautiful shoulders. Part of the guilt was mine. I got my priorities mixed up. I had something precious, and I lost it by neglect."

"That's an admission I thought you'd never make."

He grinned. "Do you retract all those remarks about my being the same will-o'-the-wisp you always knew?"

She held up both hands in surrender. "Completely. Lead me to the whipping post. Put me in the stocks." In spite of her teasing tone she was impressed by his honesty and sincerity. He *had* changed in eleven years, she thought, but she still felt cautious.

"The only place I desire to put you is in bed. Mine."

"Back to that, are we?"

"We never left it."

"I suppose not. You never could control your appetites."

"Neither could you. The memory of it has given me many sleepless nights."

"According to the papers, it was football injuries that plagued you, not lust."

"What do they know?"

The waitress brought their steaks, which were steaming and juicy and almost as big as that suitcase Amanda had mentioned. For the rest of the meal they concentrated on food and small talk. Between them, however, even small talk was not insignificant. Every phrase had a double meaning, and every word was a reminder of the past. When they noted that there would be no white Christmas for Greenville again that year, they both remembered one long ago. They'd kept each other warm by cuddling in front of the fire in Tanner's library. With all the Donovans gone, they'd made love repeatedly, watching the fascinating play of firelight across their bare skin. When they talked of music, they each recalled the first time they'd ever sung together. It had been at the wedding of the high-school drama teacher and the minister of music at Riverside. From that day they'd known they were fated to be together. Both of them had known that the harmony they created in song would carry over into lovemaking and marriage.

The nostalgia, remembered but not spoken, made them gentle with each other. They left the restaurant, arm in arm, and Tanner drove to Amanda's house. He didn't press for more than a sweet good-night kiss, and she didn't insist that he take back the jewelry.

As Tanner drove away and Amanda went inside, both vowed to themselves that tomorrow would be another day. He was planning for their future together, and she was trying to accept the reality of their future apart.

The next morning Amanda woke up reluctantly as usual, squinting at the unwelcome morning through one eye and hoping she was wrong about the sun peeping through her window. Somewhere in the distance she heard music. Her crazy neighbor singing as he went to get the morning paper, she thought. She reached for her clock. it showed a full fifteen minutes till the alarm would ring. Groaning, she pulled the covers over her head, clock and all. She couldn't believe she'd ruined fifteen good minutes of sleep by waking up.

The music seemed louder, more persistent, and it wasn't coming from next door; it was right under her window. She stuck her head out from under the covers and listened. The song was "Nobody Does It Better," and the singer was Tanner Donovan.

She pulled the covers back over her head and mumbled, "I should cover him with chunky peanut butter and feed him to the birds. I ought to string him up and hang him from the tree at City Hall." The sound of music penetrated her warm cocoon of blankets, and she grinned in spite of herself. "Audacious man. Maybe he'll give up and go away." As she lay there waiting from him to go, it occurred to her that she wanted to see him. *Had* to see him. Not for any romantic reasons, she rationalized, but she needed to look at him—just a glimpse, or maybe two or three. She didn't know why. She didn't want to know why.

She hopped out of bed, scattering blankets hither and yon, and hurried to the window. Without thinking, she threw it open and leaned out.

Tanner was there, dressed in his white cowboy

outfit, one boot propped on the front fender of his car. Nobody had the flamboyance and style of Tanner Donovan, she decided.

Her delighted peal of laughter sent a cardinal into flight.

"You scalawag. You're going to wake everybody in the neighborhood with that racket."

Tanner gave new meaning to the Southern expression, "rared back." He didn't lean back; he rared. Mandy felt as if she'd discovered Christmas for the first time, and she knew that one glance wouldn't be enough.

"And you're going to start a riot in that scanty pink lace thing you're wearing. I'll probably have to challenge every man in the neighborhood to a duel."

She reached over and pulled the curtain around her body. "It's all your fault. Go away."

"Invite me in. I'm bearing gifts."

"I'm not accepting any more jewelry from you."

She didn't notice her slip of the tongue, but Tanner did. She wouldn't take any more, but he'd be willing to bet she'd keep the ones she had. He knew that if he put them on her, she wouldn't be able to give them back. Amanda loved jewelry—the more elaborate, the better.

"How about food?"

She could imagine what goodies he'd brought from Anna's kitchen, but she stood firm. "No."

"Gingerbread." He held the gingerbread to his nose and sniffed. "Heavenly."

She licked her lips. "That's sneaky."

"That's smart. I've discovered the way to your heart, Amanda. Are you going to let me in?"

"You wouldn't consider leaving it on the doorstep?"

"It's a gingerbread man. He'd feel abandoned."

"All right, then, but you can stay only long enough to give it to me."

"I'm in love with a greedy woman."

"None of your tricks, Tanner. Promise?"

He held up his hand. "On my word of honor."

She put on her bright pink silk robe and hurried to the door. Tanner looked twice as good today as he had the day before. She supposed it had to do with the gingerbread he held in his hand.

She opened the door wide.

He stepped through. Holding the gingerbread in one hand, he pulled her against his chest with the other.

"I dreamed of how luscious you'd be with your hair tumbled from sleep. You've exceeded my wildest expectations."

"Tanner, you said on your honor."

"I have no honor." He tightened his hold. "You make me forget all my plans to woo you properly. I want you." He bent down and skimmed his lips down her cheeks, around her jawline. His mouth hovered close to hers, so close that she almost could taste him. "I want to take this bit of silk off and see your body."

"No, Tanner . . . don't." Her words came out in small, breathless spurts.

"I remember every delicious inch of you; those gorgeous legs, that tiny mole inside your right thigh, your rosy nipples and the way I could make them hard by looking at them." His gaze held hers as he moved his hand around and brushed her slowly, sensuously, through her silk robe. "The way they are now. You want me. Say you do."

"Yes . . . oh, yes."

His hand continued its erotic massage. "I love you, Mandy. I want to marry you. And I don't know if I have the patience for a long courtship."

"No." She could barely speak the word, but she knew she had to. "Please don't, Tanner."

"I believe you love me, Mandy. Can you deny it?"

His hands were still on her, doing remarkable, wonderful things. She could see so deep into his eyes, she imagined she'd glimpsed his soul.

"It doesn't matter anymore."

"It matters—to both of us."

"Forget what I once felt for you, or what I feel for you now. We can never have a future together. Claude—"

"Will never come between us again." His expression became fierce. "Dammit, Mandy. Say you love me."

Her laugh was shaky. "You're wasting your time with me."

His mouth covered hers swiftly, greedily. She leaned into him, fitting every inch of herself to his muscular body. Her emotions were in a frenzy because she knew that what they shared—something so wonderful, so right, so good—had to end.

His lips left hers.

"Not yet. Oh, Tanner. Please. Kiss me again."

He took her mouth again, but this time with an aching tenderness and an unbearable sweetness. She felt as if he were wrapping rainbows around her heart. The brightness radiated through her, and she caught a glimpse of what it would be like to be his wife. He was a man who knew how to cherish a woman.

What she couldn't say to him earlier, she spoke through the kiss. She loved him. Now and always. No matter how many years or how many miles came between them, she would never be free of Tanner Donovan. With all her heart she wished Claude would vanish, would disappear as if he had never existed. She knew she was being foolish and selfish and childish, but there was no other way they could be happy together. The knowledge shattered her.

Tanner held her long after the kiss had ended. Tucked close to him, she felt secure and needed and loved. She rested her head against his shoulder and let the feelings wash over her.

She placed a soft kiss on his neck. "I have to go to work."

"I know, love."

"You have to release me." Her voice was gentle with love.

"Only temporarily." He eased his hold. "Your breakfast, my darling." He placed the gingerbread boy in her hand. "It goes well with a tall glass of milk. I want the mother of my children to be healthy."

"I can accept your food and your friendship, Tanner, but nothing more."

He smiled. It was a little-boy-trying-to-be-brave look that made her want to cuddle his head to her breast.

"I have four older brothers who've all wooed and won the women they love. It would be a shame to break the Donovan track record."

"I know losing is not your style, Tanner, but you'll just have to get used to the idea."

"Mandy, love, when my brothers get through tutoring me on the finer points of courtship, you won't be able to say no."

She remembered him as a little boy, bringing bitter weeds to his mother. Saying no to him made her feel like a miserly old hypocrite. Lord, she thought, what a mess life could be sometimes.

She held out her hand. "Good-bye, Tanner. Please thank Anna for the gingerbread."

"It was her pleasure—and mine."

He kissed her hand. "Remember the milk,

Mandy. And by the way, there's a note in your kitchen I think you should see."

He left, whistling.

Amanda stood in the doorway watching until she could no longer see his car. Then she went to her kitchen. The note, propped on her table, was the first thing she saw. He must have put it there Monday night, she decided, after she had taunted him with her striptease act.

She laid the gingerbread aside, picked up the note, and read. "This time, Amanda, you'll choose me." She felt tears forming. Tearing the note in half, she threw it in the wastebasket. "I won't cry." She shut her eyes. The tears eased out from the corners of her lids and inched down her cheeks. She rubbed them away with her hands. "I *will not* cry." Her gaze fell on the gingerbread boy. She remembered what Tanner had said about the milk and the children. She covered her mouth with her hands as the sobs shook her. "Oh, Lord, Tanner. Am I wrong?"

She choked back her sobs and stood very still, listening.

The silence in the house mocked her.

Maxine had already opened the shop when she arrived.

"I'm sorry I'm late."

"Ten minutes is not late. It's common sense. Especially when you look like you do."

Amanda placed the gingerbread boy and the half-pint of milk on her desk. "How's that?"

"Beautiful but pale. Are you sick?"

"No. Just tired. I haven't been sleeping well. It's the Christmas rush, I guess."

"I won't burden you with my opinion on that subject." Maxine took a stack of petticoats out of a trunk and began to hang them in a massive walnut armoire. "I'm glad Dorothy and Janet are coming in tomorrow to work the rest of the Christmas season. They love it, and we need their help."

Amanda sat down at her desk and began to eat. The gingerbread was spicy and the milk was cold. She tried to clear her mind, but as she nibbled first on the head and then on the arms of the gingerbread boy, she thought of all the Donovan grandchildren crowding into Anna's kitchen, waiting for a hot batch fresh from the oven.

She put the thought firmly out of her mind.

"I'm glad you're changing the petticoats. They show up better over there."

"I thought so, myself. Think what a clever woman Wilford is getting."

"I agree." She ate the last crumb of gingerbread and tossed the empty milk carton into the wastebasket. It was amazing how much better she felt. She stood up, smoothing her blue wool skirt and sweater. "Time to open shop."

They were busy until well after lunch. It seemed to them that half the women in Greenville had chosen Wednesday morning to shop. The stock of velvet and satin dresses dwindled, and even the wedding gown they'd bought at an estate auction in Vicksburg was sold.

"Shall we bring out the one you got in Savannah?" Maxine asked.

It was Amanda's favorite, a shimmering concoction of antique satin and lace with intricate beading that today's seamstresses would never attempt. The dress was a perfect size eight. Her size.

"No. Let's wait on that one."

Maxine smiled but said nothing.

They took advantage of the lull to bring out some Victorian blouses and make minor repairs.

They had moved their chairs close to the window to be nearer to the light.

Maxine was the first to see the lavender car coming up the street.

"Would you look at that?"

It was a 1967 El Dorado Cadillac convertible with the top down. Two Texas longhorns were attached to the front fender. The woman driving it looked like a Gypsy. Her wild black hair was blowing in the wind, and the arm she had hanging over the side was covered with bangle bracelets.

Amanda's mouth fell open. In the passenger seat was Tanner Donovan. Her heart did a quick rhumba, then settled into a painful thud. She knew she should be relieved that he had finally given up on her, but she wasn't. Furthermore, she wanted to shove that Gypsy woman out of the front seat and into the dirt.

"It didn't take him long, did it?" she muttered.

The car came closer. Crowds of curious onlookers blocked their view. Maxine stood up so she could see.

"I might have known. It's Hallie Donovan."

Amanda felt as if she might float off to Mars. "Hallie? Are you sure?"

"Yes. I should have known. They say all she took from her divorce to that rich man was the lavender El Dorado Cadillac and two dogs. Can you imagine that? Just an old car and two dogs. As a matter of fact, that's them in the backseat."

Once Amanda had spotted Tanner, she hadn't noticed the dogs. She stood up and peered over Maxine's shoulder. Two great Danes, looking as big as Shetland ponies, were sitting on the backseat, their upright ears saluting the December breeze.

Amanda smiled as she watched Hallie swing the car into a parking place without checking her speed. Hallie always had been a wild one, more like Tanner than any of his other brothers or sisters. They even looked alike; both had dark hair and silver eyes, and both were tall, handsome, and reeking of self-confidence as they descended from the car, acting as if riding around in a lavender Cadillac with bullhorns on the front was a natural thing to do in Greenville.

"Life will never be dull for those two," Maxine remarked.

Amanda silently wished she could find out.

Tanner stood beside the car, looking across the street directly at her shop, while he waited for Hallie to give orders to her dogs. When Hallie leaned into the car to talk to the animals, every man within view almost had a heart attack. Her trim rear, perched high and tight on her long coltish legs, was encased in jeans so snug, they looked as if they had been painted on. To make matters worse, she talked with her whole body, jiggling her bracelets and her derriere with equal aplomb.

A crowd the size of the Mormon Tabernacle Choir gathered around the Donovans, impeding their progress as they started toward Amanda's shop. Tanner and Hallie dispensed handshakes and hugs as if they had invented them.

The shop sizzled with energy when they stepped through the door.

Hallie swooped down on Amanda, gave her a quick bear hug, then leaned back to look at her. "Since I got home Tanner has talked of nothing but you. I insisted on seeing your shop."

Tanner laughed. "Hallie's up to mischief, Amanda. Pay no attention to a word she says."

Hallie's bracelets jingled as she waved him aside. "Go over there and spend some of your money, Tanner. Buy me a present. I want to talk to Amanda."

"Don't be bossy, Hallie. It's unbecoming in a lady."

"I'm no lady," Hallie rejoined, chuckling.

Maxine had taken refuge behind the jewelry counter, and Amanda finally managed to catch her breath and get a word in edgewise.

"I'm glad to see you, Hallie." She'd be glad to see the devil if he had Tanner in tow, she decided. Her gaze swung around the shop till she found him. He looked up from a stack of Victorian blouses and winked. "You're home for the holidays?"

"I'm home for as long as the spirit moves me. Wolfgang and Ludwig and I are just batting around the country, looking for fun and adventure."

"Wolfgang and Ludwig?"

"My Great Danes. They like classical music." Hallie hooked her thumbs through her belt loops, tipped back on her heels, and gave Amanda an appraising look. "Tanner was right. You're even more beautiful now than when the two of you were engaged."

Tanner caught Amanda's eye and blew her a kiss. Hallie didn't miss a thing.

"Are you planning to marry this cocky brother of mine?"

"No." Amanda avoided Tanner's gaze when she spoke. She wondered if Hallie had guessed his intentions or if he had told her. Probably the latter. It wouldn't surprise her if he hired a plane and wrote it in the sky. He never could do anything the ordinary way.

"That's smart." Hallie's eyes twinkled with mischief. Amanda knew that Hallie idolized Tanner, always had, even when she was a pigtailed first-grader and Tanner was in junior high. She was also quite a prankster and loved playing the devil's advocate. "Tanner has too much money. Men with too much money can be a pain in the—"

"Association," Tanner said, cutting in smoothly. He was having a hard time holding back his laughter. "Hallie believes in guilt by association. Men with bank accounts of more than six figures are automatically guilty of all sorts of wicked deeds, including keeping their women in gilded cages." He left Maxine at the cash register totaling a huge stack of merchandise, and crossed the room to Amanda and Hallie. Wrapping them both in a bear hug, he continued. "Hallie enjoys rabble-rousing. Actually she's embarrassed to say what she really thinks about me. She thinks I'm wonderful. Just as you do. It's a pity that both of you are too shy to say it."

Amanda and Hallie laughed.

"What did I tell you? A pain in the—"

"Arrogant," Amanda said, "He was always arrogant."

"Listen to the two of them, Maxine. The slings and arrows of love. They're wild about me."

"Everybody is, Tanner, and if they're not, they ought to be ashamed of themselves." Maxine waved her arm over the stack of Victorian blouses and petticoats, velvet dresses, and beaded gowns. "Do you want all this gift-wrapped?"

"Yes, please. In one big box."

Hallie whooped for joy. "For me, Tanner? You got all that for me?"

"Weren't you the one who wrote a letter to Santa and slipped it under my door not more than ten minutes after you arrived in Greenville?" He released her and tousled her hair. "For a woman who vows to hate money, you sure do love the things money can buy. You're a fraud, Hallie. Lovable but a fraud."

She laughed. "Watch what you say, buster. I'll sic all my older brothers on you." Suddenly she stood very still, cupping one hand around her ear.

"Do I hear a noise? It sounds like the rushing of little airplane wings." She took Amanda's hand and tugged her toward the door. "Come on, Amanda. We don't want to miss this."

Tanner followed them and circled his arms around Amanda's waist from behind. "My baby sister was supposed to be subtle. Nonetheless, she got the job done." He rested his chin on Amanda's hair. "Look up, love. I've planned a surprise for you."

Spider Hendrix's yellow crop-dusting plane flew low over Washington Street, trailing a huge banner across the sky: "Amanda, I love you. Tanner." Before the banner was out of sight, Spider dipped and turned back toward the antique shop. A curious crowd blocked Amanda's view.

Tanner walked her through the door. "We don't want to miss the show." He lifted her to his shoulder with no effort at all. With one hand supporting her bottom and the other holding her legs, he grinned up at her. "Comfortable?"

She affectionately smoothed his hair. "Oh, Tanner. This is too much."

"Is that good or bad?"

"I'm not sure." Shading her eyes against the afternoon sun, she tracked the plane until it was out of sight. The banner proclaimed to the entire city what Tanner had been professing since the night before. "That was a good show, Tanner. It'll give everybody something to talk about besides Christmas presents and the weather."

"It wasn't just a show, Mandy." He caressed her legs. "I meant it. I mean it."

Before she could argue with him, she heard the roar that signaled the return of the plane. Looking up, she saw not Spider's plane but the red crop duster belonging to Toad Ellis. The banner streaking along behind him declared, "Marry me, Amanda. Say yes."

There was a collective sigh from the crowd on the sidewalk.

Perched on Tanner's shoulder, Amanda heard everything that was said.

"Isn't that romantic?"

"Nobody but Tanner Donovan would propose like that."

"Did she say yes?"

"She'd be crazy not to."

"After all these years! Who says love doesn't conquer all?"

As the plane became a speck in the sky, the crowd dispersed, all still talking.

Amanda brushed a telltale tear from her eye and put a brave smile on her face.

"Would you put me down now so I can go back inside, Tanner?"

He lowered her until her feet touched the sidewalk, letting her slide against his body so that every inch of her felt branded by him.

"Mandy?"

He had such a look of happy anticipation on his face that she wanted to cry. How could she deny her love for this man? she wondered. But she knew she must, for both their sakes.

Lifting her hands, she touched his face. "It was a beautiful gesture. Thank you."

"You're welcome."

He waited. She could feel the tension in his body. "Please, Tanner. I can't marry you. It would be a mistake."

"Do you love me, Amanda?"

Closing her eyes, she took a deep breath. He deserved the truth. "Yes." She opened her eyes and saw the joy in his face. "Yes, Tanner. I can't seem to help myself. I've fallen in love with you all over again."

"That's enough for now." His lips touched hers as gently as spring dew on new leaves. "I want to marry you, Mandy. And I'm not a patient man. I won't sit back and wait. I'll pursue you to the gates of hell, if that's what it takes to convince you you're wrong."

"Somehow I thought you would."

"You're smiling, Amanda. I take that as a sure sign that I'll win."

"You take everything as a sign that you'll win."

He shrugged. "What can I say? Winning's my style."

She patted his cheek. "Not this time, Tanner. This is not a game; it's life. We nearly destroyed each other once. I won't let that happen again."

He bent down and kissed her, swiftly and hard. "I'll see you at the altar."

As if she'd been waiting for a cue, Hallie came through the door. With a final wave and a smile, she and Tanner crossed the street and drove off in the lavender Cadillac.

Life with Tanner surely would be fun, Amanda thought. Her brave smile was sad around the edges as she went back into her shop.

Maxine was standing beside a brass hat rack near the window. "That was the most romantic proposal I've ever seen. Imagine proclaiming his love with the whole town as witnesses."

Amanda put her hand on the forlorn spot right over her heart. "Maxine, do you mind if we don't talk about this right now?"

"Sure. There's always work to be done around here. In fact, I hear three frayed dresses calling my name." Her step was jaunty as she started toward the back room. "Lead me to a needle."

Amanda's conscience smote her. She figured that

lately she'd been about as much fun as a case of indigestion. In her zeal to keep Tanner at bay she'd probably run off all her friends, Maxine included.

"Maxine, do you remember that time in sixth grade when you and I were so glum?"

"That time we both made C's on our spelling tests because we couldn't spell discombobulate and disestablishmentarianism?"

"That's the time. I still can't, can you?"

"Heck, no. And it never has mattered one way or the other." Maxine's grin was devilish. "Unless it caused me to lose my second husband. He always was a stickler about things like that."

"You recall how we got ourselves out of the dumps, don't you?"

"You mean . . ." Maxine's eyes got big and sparkly.

"Precisely. Man the fort. I'm going to Tudberry's."

Grabbing her sweater, Amanda raced out the door and down the street. Everything about Tudberry's looked the same as it had when Amanda was a child, even the display window. The little red wagon and the red fire truck were shinier, but she'd swear that the dusty old teddy bear with the faded ribbon was the same one she'd seen there twenty some years ago.

Mr. Tudberry was a hidebound traditionalist. Knowing that some things never changed made Amanda feel good.

She passed through the dimly lit aisles of dolls and dart boards and baseball bats and tricycles, until she came to the place she sought—Mr. Tudberry's sports center. It could be called a sports center only in the loosest sense. Actually it was a mixture of sporting equipment piled together around an old poster of Esther Williams in one of her movies.

Mr. Tudberry himself was in the center of all the confusion. With his tufts of white eyebrows sticking up like an owl's, his glasses almost falling off his skinny nose, and his brown wool sweater hanging on his body as if on a skeleton, he looked exactly as she remembered.

"Well, now." He always greeted his customers by rubbing his hands together, and if he ever said anything besides "Well, now," the whole town would consider it a miracle.

The familiar routine comforted Amanda.

"Merry Christmas, Mr. Tudberry. How are you?"

"Can't complain." He always said that, too, right before he did complain. "Of course, the old arthritis is actin' up. Must be some bad weather comin' on. And the dentist wants to pull all my teeth and give me a false set. Can't stand the thought of the dad-blamed things. Ever since Clarence got his, he can't eat a thing except infernal milk and cornbread."

"I'm sorry to hear that."

"We all have our aches and pains. The price of getting old, I guess. Well, now. What can I do for you?"

"Do you still have hoola hoops?"

When Mr. Tudberry chuckled, he sounded like a couple of turkey gobblers locked in a closet. "Nobody's asked for hoola hoops in a month of Sundays." He began to rummage through an assortment of basketball hoops and tennis nets and badminton rackets. "Nope. Don't get much call for them anymore. Not since that craze. When was it? Sixties? Seventies? Whoops. Here they are. If they'da been a snake, they'da bit me." He held up a fluorescent orange plastic hoop.

Amanda bought two hoola hoops, said good-bye to Mr. Tudberry, and hurried back to her shop.

Four customers were browsing leisurely through

the racks of blouses. She leaned the hoola hoops against the brass hat rack, then went about her business of selling.

As soon as the last customer was out the door, she brought out the hoops.

"Here, Maxine. One for me and one for you."

Maxine hooted. "You don't expect me to use that thing, do you? I'm likely to throw my back out of joint."

Amanda slipped the hoop around hips. "Where's your sense of adventure? One never forgets how to do this." She began gyrating in a remembered rhythm. The hoop made three shaky revolutions around her hips, then skittered to the floor. She picked it up and started again. "There's nothing to it, Maxine. Watch this." This time the hoop stayed up for six revolutions.

"I'm impressed, Amanda. But then, your equipment's better than mine."

Amanda picked her hoop off the floor. "The hoola hoop?"

"No. The hips. Mine are carrying about six pounds of extra baggage." She stepped into her hoop and did a brave bump and grind. The hoop banged her toes on the way to the floor. "Ouch. Probably chipped my polish, to boot."

"Trouble is, you don't have the rhythm." Amanda got her hoop going. "We used to sing. Remember?" She started singing.

"Greenville, are you ready for this?" Maxine said, joining in now.

They laughed and gyrated and sang every old "doo-wah" song they could think of. A few customers who drifted in thought they were crazy, but that didn't bother Amanda. The hoola hoops had served their purpose. They'd helped her put Tanner out of her mind for an entire afternoon.

• • •

While Amanda was hoola hooping, Hallie was driving through the town in a manner that made even Tanner's hair stand on end.

"You burned rubber back there at the stoplight, Hallie. It's a wonder Lard Pritchard doesn't put you under arrest."

Her bracelets jangled as she leaned over and patted his cheek. "Smile, brother. I'm just taking a little tour of the dear old hometown."

"You're going so fast, you can't see a thing."

"I like adventure." She whizzed past a McDonald's at such a speed the golden arches looked like a smear of butter.

"If you don't mind, get me home in one piece. I don't plan to walk down the aisle to the altar in a body cast."

"Love's turned you into an old sourpuss." She turned the Cadillac around—on two wheels, Tanner speculated—and headed toward home. Hallie pretended to pout, but Tanner knew she was faking. She was never upset, and besides that, when they passed Coot Sampson's farm, she forgot she was supposed to be mad at him and laughed out loud.

"Hey, Tanner, remember when I use to date Coot Sampson?"

"How can I forget it? You took the label off a tube of Ben Gay and told him it was love gel. He stayed out of school a whole week."

"Served him right for trying to grope me in the oleander bush." As the car shot around the last curve toward home, Hallie blasted the horn. It played "The Eyes of Texas Are Upon You." Then she skidded the last thirty feet, sending gravel spewing up behind them.

Tanner laughed. Hallie loved entrances, and she sure knew how to make them. She was a Donovan through and through.

He took her hand and helped her from the car. "Come on, Hallie. It looks like my surprise has arrived."

The surprise was parked near the barn, a luxurious horse van, watched over anxiously by a young man with hair the color of straw and ears as big as Arkansas.

Tanner shook his hand. "Johnson. You made good time."

"Yep." Johnson tipped back on his boots and tried to look straight at his employer, but his eyes kept straying toward Hallie. "You said you wanted Napoleon as soon as possible. I didn't see any need to lollygag around. He's already unloaded and in the barn."

The three of them walked through the barn door. Inside was a gorgeous thoroughbred, a Tennessee walking horse with a long, finely muscled back and a coat that gleamed like black onyx in the sunlight.

Tanner patted the horse's muzzle. "What do you think, Hallie?"

"I think I'm in love. Is this the horse that has won so many trophies?"

"The same. Amanda used to have a romantic notion about riding off into the sunset. Somehow old Josephine didn't seem to fit the bill."

Hallie put her face on the horse's shiny neck. "Tanner, if Robert had been more like you, I might have stayed married to him—in spite of his money."

If he hadn't been so attuned to his sister's moods, he might not have heard the breathless catch in her voice. It was the first time since her divorce that she'd shown the slightest vulnerability. A great protective urge welled up inside Tanner. "Would you like to ride him?"

"Would I?" She flung herself at her brother and

squeezed him around the chest. "You're a sweet-heart."

As Tanner saddled Napoleon, he imagined sitting in the saddle, putting the horse into a canter. He could almost feel the high, rolling motion beneath him, sense the twisting and turning of horse's back feet. To his mind the Tennessee walking horse had always been the most sensuous breed. Their smooth, graceful gait was almost like being rocked in a cradle of love.

As Tanner gave Hallie a leg up, he thought about Amanda, about riding with her on the horse. Desire ripped through him.

He glanced down at his watch. It had been only an hour since he had seen her, and already he wanted to grab time by the neck and pull it screaming toward the night. He considered running all the way back to the shop, writing her a check for the business, locking the doors, and carrying her off into the sunset. But he supposed that wouldn't work. He'd have to learn to wait like a sensible man.

"The devil's pitchfork!" he muttered.

Hallie leaned down from the saddle. "Did you say something?"

"Nothing worth repeating. Have a good ride."

Seven

Amanda decided a long walk in the moonlight would help her forget everything—the planes zooming across the sky that afternoon, Tanner's proposal, and most of all, her love for him. Dressed in jeans and a sweater, she left her house and started down the block.

Although the temperature had dropped, fifty degrees was warm for December. There was no wind, and the stars hung in the sky like tinsel on a Christmas tree. It was jeans-and-sweater weather, football weather. Amanda kicked at a twig. Why did everything have to make her think of Tanner? She missed him so much, she had to hug herself to hold in the ache.

She lengthened her stride, keeping her mind busy by checking off the houses as she walked. She passed the Crumpets', who were sitting in front of their picture window with the blinds open, watching *Wheel of Fortune* as if their lives depended on keeping the TV set warm. The Rogers' house was dark. They'd probably gone to Minneapolis to visit their daughter for the holidays. Music poured forth from the Grahams', "Rudolph

the Red-nosed Reindeer," amplified loud enough
so that the grandmother, who hadn't heard anything since Pearl Harbor, could feel the vibrations
and tap her feet. Amanda made a mental note to
take Grandma Graham a box of those peppermint
bonbons she loved. The Pickens children were in
their front yard playing a last game of hide-and-
seek before their parents called them in from the
dark.

"Hey, 'Manda," Sue Lynn called. "Santie comin'
to see you?"

Amanda stopped on the sidewalk and spoke to
the six-year-old. "I hope so, Sue Lynn. Do you and
Richard have your stockings hung?"

"Yes, ma'am." Eight-year-old Richard ran up and
tugged her hand. "Wanna see?"

"Yes. That would be lovely." The Pickens children tucked their sticky hands into hers and led
her into their house. She properly admired their
stockings, politely took a candy cane they offered,
chatted briefly with Martha Sue and Eddie Wayne,
then went back outside to continue her walk.

She was halfway down the next block before she
noticed her cheeks were wet. Sniffing, she rubbed
her face with the back of her hand and sat down
on the curb to eat her candy cane.

That's how Tanner found her.

"Is this a private party, or can anyone join in?"

She looked up to see him sitting on an amazing
black stallion with a silver-studded saddle and
bridle that would put Roy Rogers to shame. The
moonlight reflected off the tears on her cheeks.

"The horse is invited."

He slid off and sat down beside her. "You're
beautiful when you cry." He pulled a handkerchief
from his pocket, put one arm around her, and
dabbed her tears away. "What's wrong, love?"

The sweet croon of his voice undid her. "It's this candy cane." She held the sticky treat aloft.

"What about the candy cane?" He caressed her back as he gently prompted her.

She buried her face in his shirt and clung to him, heedless of the peppermint. "Oh, Tanner." She squeezed him tighter, squashing candy juice against his back. "Christmas is for children. When I see little stockings hung by the chimney, I mourn for the children I never had."

"We'll have children. Lots of them."

She lifted her face, her eyes wet with tears. "We could have had children, Tanner. I find that very sad."

"Don't mourn the past, Amanda. Think of the future. We'll have so many little Donovans, there won't be room by the chimney to hang all the stockings."

She smiled up at him. "You make it sound possible. But then, you were always an irrepressible optimist."

He ruffled her hair. "Feel better?"

"Yes. I don't know why but I do. You always had the knack for curing my blues."

"Good. How about sharing that candy cane?"

There was some resistance as she pulled it away from his chamois shirt. Green fuzz clung to the sticky candy.

"I'm afraid I've ruined your shirt."

"That's a small sacrifice for the privilege of holding you in my arms." He took the candy, stood up, and tossed it toward the garbage can on the corner. They heard a metallic ping as it hit the bottom of the can. Taking the handkerchief, he knelt beside her and carefully cleaned her hand.

The moment was sweeter to her than all the times he'd kissed her with fierceness and passion. She cherished everything about him—his tenderness, his compassion, his kindness. The Tanner she loved was the same fun-loving, passionate man she'd loved so long ago, but there was more to him, so much more.

With him kneeling before her in the moonlight, she gave in to her feelings. She knew they'd never share the kind of future that he envisioned for them—marriage and children and stockings by the fire—because Claude was still between them. Tanner had managed to push him to the back of his mind, but forgetting a problem wasn't the same as facing it. What she and Tanner could have, though, was love. They could seize the time he had left in Greenville and make it their own. If he asked, and she knew he would, she'd go to him willingly and without regrets.

And after he was gone, she'd have beautiful memories.

"All done." Tanner kissed her hand. "Now, how about a ride in the moonlight?"

Amanda stood up and patted the magnificent animal's velvety muzzle. "Where did you get him?"

"From my stables in Dallas. After my experience with old Josephine, I called Johnson and had him bring Napoleon out in the horse van."

"He's beautiful. But, Tanner, what in the world are you doing riding on the city streets?"

"I drove him out to your house in the van. When you weren't home and I saw your car in the garage, I guessed you'd gone for a walk. So Napoleon and I came to your rescue."

"I don't suppose it ever occurred to you to wait at my house?"

"Never." He boosted her into the saddle and mounted behind her. "This is so much more romantic, don't you think?"

She leaned against him. "Hmmm. Just my style.

I've always wanted to ride into the sunset on a horse."

"I'd supply the sun if I could. Will the moon do?"

She looked up into the sky and laughed. "You did that just for me, Tanner? You commanded the moon to shine?"

"I have connections in high places." He turned Napoleon toward Amanda's house, guiding him carefully on the dark city street. "Are you warm enough?"

"Yes. You create lots of body heat."

"I can think of a number of ways to create more."

"Would I enjoy them?"

"You used to."

"That was so long ago, I barely remember."

"Perhaps I should give you a refresher course."

"On the horse?"

"Why, Miss Lassiter, what a bawdy suggestion."

"I aim to shock."

"You delight."

Tanner reined Napoleon in next to the van. "I've planned a moonlight ride beside the river, Amanda. Do you need a warmer sweater?"

"As the old saying goes, 'I've got my love to keep me warm.' "

"Yes, you do. And always will. Remember that."

Tanner dismounted, swung Amanda from the saddle, and guided Napoleon into the plush horse van. It was an easy task, since both horse and rider had done it many times before.

They drove south of town until they came to one of their favorite old haunts, a secluded place beside a bend in the river. The moon painted a luminous path across the water, and the hardwood trees lifted their bare branches to touch the face of the sky. All the night creatures were tucked deep into their warm burrows and hollows. Even

the fish sought refuge deep below the iridescent
water. The winter silence was eloquent and beautiful.

Tanner and Amanda kept the silence as he unloaded Napoleon. Mounted on the horse's back,
they gazed across the river. Peace soaked into
their souls.

"I love this place," Tanner said quietly.

"So do I."

"It's the perfect spot to tell you all that's in my
heart."

"Didn't you do that this afternoon?"

"That sideshow with the planes and banners?"

"Yes."

"That was merely to get your attention."

"You did."

"A real proposal should be more romantic. And
private."

"Tanner, please. You know how I feel."

"Hear me out, Amanda."

His voice was quiet and rich with feeling, but it
held the steel edge of command that she couldn't
ignore. She half turned in the saddle so she could
see his face. All the love he felt for her was there.

"Loving you again has given me new purpose,
Amanda. The public sees me as a man who has
everything—good health, fame, wealth. They don't
see the emptiness, the lonesome times when I
rattle around in my big old house with nobody
but the staff to know or care whether I'm dead or
alive."

She started to protest, but he shushed her with
a finger on her lips.

"I know I have a family—wonderful parents,
brothers and sisters and sisters-in-law and nieces
and nephews—who loves me and all with private
lives that don't include me. What I'm missing is a

special someone to call my own, a woman who will share my life, bear my children."

He cupped her face and gazed at her in silence that echoed all the things he'd said. "You are that woman, Amanda. You've always been that woman."

"Thank you, Tanner. That was beautiful." She pressed his hands, holding them close against her face so that she could feel the strength and power of him. "I love you. That's all I can give you right now. You are a special man, a man who deserves the truth. And the truth is, I'm more cautious than you, and more practical. I don't think life is as simple as getting married and living happily ever after."

"We could, you know."

"When you say it like that, I want to believe you."

"Believe me."

She reached out and traced his face with her fingertips. The mesmerizing gleam in his eyes spoke to her, beckoned to her, seduced her. She leaned into him and lightly outlined his lips with her tongue.

"You tempt me so," she whispered. "But I cannot marry you."

"Our time will come, Mandy. I promise you that."

With a quick flick of the reins Tanner sent Napoleon thundering along the river. Sand spewed up behind them, silver plumes of fairy dust in the moonlight.

The power of horse and man flowed through Amanda. On the wild gallop down the river they merged in her mind until Tanner and his stallion became one and the same, a magnificent creation pulsing with the electrifying force of nature. Raw passion burned in the winter night. Amanda felt its heat. Every fiber in her body responded to Tanner, cried out "Yes" to him.

Tanner reined the stallion to a halt. He dismounted and reached up for Amanda, setting her down and pulling her swiftly into his arms. "Mandy?"

"Yes, Tanner. Oh, Lord, yes."

His lips were on hers, frenzied, wild, greedy. With their hungry mouths on each other she ripped his shirt aside, sending buttons flying across the sand. She circled her arms around him under the shirt, pulling him so close that she thought the pounding of his heartbeat was her own.

With an urgency that comes from passion too long denied, they fell to the sand. Their hands tore open zippers, pushed aside restraining fabric, until they were joined.

Only then did the urgency begin to subside.

"Mandy!" Tanner crushed her in his embrace. "You feel so good. Oh, Lord, I've wanted this for so long."

"So have I." Their hips began a small rhythm. She spoke in ragged spurts. "Always I remembered how you felt, like thunder clothed in velvet."

"I've dreamed of you like this a thousand times, but it was never this good." His lips devoured hers as he thrust deep into her. "Baby, baby," he murmured. "You make me explode."

Amanda felt the chill sands against her back as she welcomed Tanner home. They began another wild ride, heart to heart, flesh to flesh. The pounding of water against the shoreline was tame compared to the wild, wanton rhythm of the lovers. Vocal in their loving, they murmured into each other's mouths, cried out private words of encouragement, words that only they had shared.

The chill winds blew across them, but they didn't notice, for they were wrapped in a cocoon of heat generated by their passion. They loved as only two people starving for each other could love—long and hard, driven by a desperate need to wipe out the past and bridge the empty years.

When they finally lay still in each other's arms, languid and fulfilled, Tanner's hands, and his softly crooned words, created a beautiful harmony that was like music.

"I'm glad, Tanner," she whispered. "I'm glad we loved."

"It's a new beginning for us, Amanda."

"Please don't make more of this than it is."

"Shhh. Let's not listen to reason tonight. Let's listen only to our hearts."

She snuggled closer to him. Her lips brushed across his chest. "Hmmm. Beautiful. Delicious. You are the most superbly built man I've ever known. I could spend a hundred years admiring your body." Her hands moved down his back and patted his bottom. "Cute. You always did have a cute backside."

His exuberant laughter rang out in the winter night and echoed across the river. "That's the right idea, but part of me that you're admiring so extravagantly is about to freeze off." He pulled her up and collected their scattered clothes. "Let's move this heartfelt admiration to warmer quarters. I don't intend for us to die of exposure before I get you to the altar."

They dressed quickly and mounted Napoleon. The ride back to the van was vastly different. This time they saw the bright veil of moonlight on the deep, dark water. They noted the stars decorating the trees as if they'd fallen from the sky and caught in the bare branches. They even spotted an owl, brave predator of the dark, swooping through the pine trees, its mystic cry haunting the winter night.

By mutual consent they headed to Tanner's house.

He parked the van beside the barn and led Napoleon inside. The horse neighed in appreciation of the brisk rubdown and the warm horse blanket. Tanner gave him a final pat as he guided him into his hay-scented stall.

"What a magnificent animal."

Tanner gave her a mocking smile. "Me or the horse?"

"You." She pushed aside his torn shirt and nuzzled his chest. "Does this barn still have a hayloft?"

"It does, but when all the Donovans are home, it pays to check it out first. Paul and Martie sneaked off here this afternoon shortly after they arrived, leaving me to baby-sit their two hellions." He climbed halfway up the ladder and poked his head into the loft. "All clear." Jumping down, he took a worn sign off a nail on the wall and started toward the door.

"What in the world are you doing?"

He held the sign so she could read it: OCCUPIED. She chuckled.

"Theo was the first Donovan to fall in love. After a very entertaining and educational show-and-tell out here, he made this sign."

"You didn't!"

"How do you know it was me?"

"You were always the one in trouble."

He hung the sign outside the barn door and drew it shut. "As a matter of fact, it was all perfectly innocent. Paul and I had been cleaning out the stables and decided to take a nap in the hayloft. When we woke up, it was too late to make a discreet exit. We just scrunched back behind the bales of hay and got educated. Theo didn't get upset when he found out. He even offered to make us drawings of the male and female anatomy and to give us a lecture on procreation."

She reached for him. "Come here, you. I need educating."

His eyes gleamed as he looked down at her. "This could take a while."

"I have from now till Christmas."

"I was thinking more in terms of the rest of our lives." He took her hand. "Come, Mandy. If I start kissing you now, we'll never make it up that ladder."

Anticipation zinged through them as they climbed to the loft. The soft, fragrant hay welcomed them. Tanner stroked Amanda's face and hair, watching the play of moonlight on her skin.

"This face has haunted me for years. I never could get enough of looking at you."

"Were there others, Tanner?"

"Jealous?"

"I don't know why, but I am."

"That pleases me."

"You never answered the question."

"I haven't been a monk, Amanda, but there was never another woman who could make me forget you. Nobody even came close."

"I used to wonder. Your name was linked with so many women—beautiful, famous women. I followed your career, you know. You were always in the news."

"The press tended to glamorize my life." He unbuttoned her blouse and pushed it aside. "Are you warm enough?"

"Yes. I've always found the hay quite cozy."

"Now I'm the one who's jealous. I don't like to think of you sharing the hay with some other man." He was laughing, toying with her, his black eyes gleaming with mischief and desire. She loved his playfulness. It was one of the many moods she remembered. Lovemaking would never grow dull and routine with Tanner.

She laughed with him, entering into his teasing mood.

"There was no one except—" Too late she realized what she was saying.

"Claude?"

She reached up and touched his face. She could feel the tension in his jaw. "Tanner, I'm sorry. I didn't mean to bring him between us again."

Tanner brought himself under control. He'd be damned if Claude would steal everything from him—even a joyful reunion in the loft.

"You didn't. He's not between us, and he never will be." With that staunch denial he lay down beside Amanda and gathered her into his arms. "Now, where were we?" He kissed her throat. "Here?" His lips moved down to her breasts. "Or was it here?"

Her hands tangled in his hair. "There. Oh, yes, Tanner. There."

He feasted on her, rediscovering every fine inch of her body, taking his time, stretching out the hot pleasure until he wondered why the hay hadn't caught fire. He possessed her as only a man in love could.

And she became his. He could see it, sense it, feel it. She was by turns yielding and demanding under him, her cries of pleasure echoing among the rafters of the old barn.

They gloried in their oneness, reveled in remembered touches, and delighted in newly discovered ones. They held nothing back, loving recklessly.

When the final explosion came, they sank together in the hay, hearts entangled as surely as arms and legs, fulfilled and sated at last.

He laced her fingers through his and brought

her hand up to his mouth. "I, Tanner, take thee, Amanda . . ."

"To love until Christmas is over." There was a desperate gaiety in her voice. She sat up and smoothed the dark hair off his forehead. "It will be a lovely affair, Tanner, something to cherish and to remember."

"Call it an affair. Call it an obsession. Call it whatever you like, Amanda, but it will end at the altar."

As much as she wanted it to be so, she knew he was dreaming. In an attempt to keep the mood light, she ruffled his hair. "You're as stubborn as old Josephine."

"That's one of my more lovable qualities." He sat up and reached for their clothes. "If we hurry, we might make it to bed before sunup."

"Yours or mine?"

He chuckled. "Insatiable little thing, aren't you?"

"Yes. If I live to be a hundred, I don't think I could ever get enough of you."

"Amanda, it's going to be my pleasure to try to fulfill that wanton desire."

"Wanton, am I?" She swatted his bare behind. "Just for that remark I'm thinking about making you sleep downstairs on the sofa."

"That's probably the only way I'll get any sleep. And we're going to need at least a few hours. I've promised that we'd baby-sit tomorrow. Paul and Martie want the twins out of the house while their Christmas ponies are being delivered."

"We? How did you know I'd be available?"

"Maxine."

"The little snitch." Amanda laughed.

"She told me you'll have extra help during the rest of the holidays, and I knew you wouldn't be able to resist the dynamic Donovan duo."

"Pretty sure of me, weren't you?"

"Not so sure about you, but certain about myself. I don't intend to let you out of my sight until I get you to the altar."

Since it was three o'clock in the morning, she decided not to argue. Tomorrow would be soon enough to set out the guidelines for this affair.

She and Tanner climbed into his snazzy red car. She cuddled close as he drove to her house. Going up the stairs together seemed natural, and getting into the four-poster bed felt like old times.

Before "Good night" was out of her mouth, she was asleep in Tanner's arms.

"Mandy." She felt something tickle her arm. "Mandy, love." That brought her fully awake. She opened her eyes to see Tanner leaning over her. For the first time in years she was glad to welcome the morning.

She sat up in bed and squeezed her arms around his wonderful chest. "Tanner, I'm so glad to see you, I could die. Is it morning already?"

"It is now that you're awake." He kissed her. It was simple and sweet and very precious. "I'm going to pick up the twins. If you're up to it, I'll bring them back here. If not, I'll take them to the park."

"Absolutely not!" She jumped out of bed and raced around the room, gathering her toiletries. "Gracious. I have to shower and wash the hay from my hair and make breakfast. What do they eat for breakfast? How old are they? Goodness, I don't even know their names."

Tanner lounged against the bedpost, enjoying her flushed excitement. High on her pretty cheekbones, the spots of color were almost as vibrant as her hair. Her eyes were wide and bright, and there was a lovely lilt to her voice. He thought she'd never looked more beautiful. It was the anticipation of the children coming to play that did that to her, he thought. Right then and there he silently vowed that she'd have a child of her own before next Christmas.

"Matthew and Elizabeth are four. And they've been up for hours. It's ten now. They probably had pancakes and juice at about six o'clock."

Brushing her hand through her tangled hair, she looked at him. "You're dressed." She said it like an accusation.

He laughed. "Bathed, dressed, jogged, and fed."

She moaned. "Oh, Lord, Tanner. Do you always have this much energy in the morning?"

"Always."

"Then it's a good thing I'm not planning to marry you. I'm not a morning person."

"That's all right. I love you just the way you are."

Before she could reply, he was gone. She could hear him whistling all the way down the stairs.

Matthew and Elizabeth were either angels unaware or devils in disguise. Amanda couldn't decide which. In the short space of two hours they'd built and destroyed fifteen Lego block bridges; taught Amanda three nursery-school songs, one of them naughty; asked Tanner to make it snow so they could build a snowman; and turned the den into a battleground for a game of cowboys and Indians. Tanner was now tied at the stake.

" 'Manda." Matthew looked up at her with his devastating Donovan smile. "Got any matches?"

"Tell him no," Tanner said.

"How can I ignore him? He has the Donovan charm." Amanda patted Matthew's bright blond hair. "What do you want them for, angel?"

Matthew giggled. "That's what Daddy calls Mommy. I'm not no angel. I'm a boy."

"He wants to burn Uncah Tannah at the stake, like on TV." Elizabeth, with her adorable dimples and her daddy's dark hair, caught Amanda's hand. "Don't let him burn up Uncah Tannah. I love him."

"I won't, precious."

Tanner snorted. "That's hard to believe. You gave him the rope and showed him how to tie the knot."

"Party pooper. It's only a game. Anyway, you volunteered to be the victim."

"That was to save your hide, my dear. Matthew had his eye on you."

Matthew and Elizabeth hadn't heard a word that had been said since *party pooper*. They were bouncing around the room yelling "Pahty poopah" at the top of their lungs.

"At least they've forgotten about m-a-t-c-h-e-s," Amanda said, spelling the last word.

"Don't look so smug. They're thinking of something even worse. Everything they say about preacher's kids is true."

"You can't fool me, Tanner Donovan. I know a doting uncle when I see one. You positively glow every time you look at them."

He grinned. "Caught me red-handed. Can I help it if their mother is my favorite sister-in-law?"

Matthew and Elizabeth stopped bouncing long enough to tackle their uncle.

"Let's play horse, Uncah Tannah," Matthew said.

Elizabeth clapped her hands. "Goody, goody. Let's play horse." She and her brother went into another Indian war dance, chanting, "Goody, goody."

"Oh, no." Tanner gave an exaggerated groan.

Amanda bent over him to untie the ropes. "That sounds like a lovely idea."

"Not if you're the horse."

With the ropes dangling in her hands, she leaned close and spoke softly, for his ears only. "I thought you rather enjoyed being the horse."

"It depends on the rider." His gave her a long, languid look, and with war whoops all around them, they made love with their eyes.

"Tanner, do you think these angels are ready for a nap?" He thought her smile was breathtakingly beautiful. Love and passion and joy surged through him. Amanda was *his* woman, and she wanted him.

"I'll bribe them."

Scooping them up, he put them on his shoulders and played horse all the way upstairs to bed.

Eight

The Donovan house was brimming with people, food, and laughter. Amanda sat beside the fire in the den, listening to the happy sounds. She didn't know when she had felt such contentment.

Martie Donovan, holding two steaming cups of hot chocolate, came and sat down beside her.

"I thought you might like this." Martie handed her a cup.

"I could have gotten that."

"You sound like Paul. If he had his way, I'd be sitting on a silk cushion for the entire nine months. Pregnancy mystifies him."

Martie's laugh was a silvery tinkle that complemented her bright hair and her bangle bracelets. She was a vibrant woman, still slim in spite of her condition. No wonder she's Tanner's favorite sister-in-law, Amanda thought.

"Thank you. This looks delicious." Amanda took a sip.

"It's the least I could do to repay you for baby-sitting the twins yesterday. They talked thirty minutes nonstop about the fun they had at your house."

"They're adorable. Tanner and I thoroughly enjoyed them."

"He spoils them terribly. But then, he's no worse than Paul. Paul is convinced that he's fathered the sweetest, most beautiful, most brilliant children in the whole wide world. Of course, I agree." She laughed at herself.

Amanda felt a stab of envy, and then she was ashamed of herself. But, oh, how she would love to be sitting beside this fire talking about her own children—hers and Tanner's.

"By the way," Martie continued. "Where is Tanner? Did I see him sneaking out the back door with that husband of mine?"

Amanda was grateful to change the subject. "You did. Hallie was with them."

Martie chuckled. "Then you can bet they're up to mischief."

"Probably. Tanner calls it a surprise. He told me not to budge from the fire until he comes for me. And I'm only too happy to oblige. After that lunch Anna served, I'm amazed I haven't fallen asleep."

"You're welcome to nap upstairs if you like. One of the things I love about this family is that everybody does pretty much what he or she wants to do."

"What are Jacob and Hannah doing? If I counted correctly, they are the only Donovans missing."

"You did. Jacob is ballooning somewhere over North Africa, and Hannah is in Fairbanks getting her sled dogs ready to run the Yukon Quest."

Amanda laughed. "That makes running an antique clothing store very tame work. I'm surprised Tanner doesn't run away from sheer boredom."

Martie leaned over and patted her hand. "Amanda, from the way Tanner looks at you, I'd say running away is the last thing on his mind."

"Is someone taking my name in vain?" Tanner

lounged against the doorframe, smiling. The warm family scene delighted him. There was nothing he enjoyed more than seeing the woman he loved being welcomed into the bosom of his family.

Martie rose and went to him. "Don't let Paul hear you say that." She hugged his neck.

"He's been trying to reform my wicked tongue for years." Tanner winked at Amanda over Martie's head.

"Without success, I might add." The Reverend Paul Donovan strode into the room. "Angel, when you finish charming that devil, how about charming me?"

With a squeal of delight Martie rushed into his arms. "Paul! You've been gone forever! What is this wonderful surprise? You know I adore surprises."

"I'll let Tanner tell. It's his surprise."

"Bundle up, ladies." Tanner crossed to Amanda's chair and put his hand possessively on her shoulder. "If we hurry, we can build a snowman before the snow melts."

Martie and Amanda both looked out the window.

"Snow in fifty-degree weather?" Amanda smiled up at him. "What's going on, Tanner?"

"The twins wanted a white Christmas, so I gave it to them."

"Real snow?" Martie asked.

"Yes, angel," Paul told her. "All the way from the Blue Ridge Mountains. Tanner had it brought down in two refrigerated trucks. It's on the patio now. Let's get the twins before Hallie uses it all up making snowballs."

Martie and Paul left to get their children. Tanner quickly walked across the room and shut the door. Amanda was already out of her chair and in his arms when he turned back around.

Tanner's face was against her hair. "I haven't

touched you in six hours. I'm dying inside. Rescue me."

She wound her hands into the hair at the back of his head, pulling him close. "Then whose hand was that on my knee under the table at lunch?"

"That doesn't count." His lips descended on hers, and it was a long time before they spoke. "I mean, really touched," he murmured, "as in joined together. Like this morning."

She pulled back from him and cocked her head to one side, laughing. "This morning? Did something happen this morning? I must have been asleep."

He roared with laughter. "Baby, if you can do all those tricks in your sleep, I can't wait to see what you do when you're awake."

"Mind your tongue. There's a preacher in the house."

Tanner sobered. "Yes, there is, Amanda, and nothing would thrill my brother more than to perform a wedding ceremony for us."

Amanda closed her eyes and rested her head on his shoulder. Their time together was almost over. Tomorrow would be Christmas Day. Right after the new year Tanner would be going back to Dallas. Only eight more days. It didn't seem fair. Eight days was too short a time to make up for all the years of missing Tanner Donovan.

She squeezed her arms around him so tightly, she heard his breath whoosh out.

"Does that mean yes, Amanda?"

"No. It means I love you, and although you aren't gone, I'm missing you already."

"I haven't gone yet, Amanda. And you'd be surprised at what can happen in eight days." Cradling her tenderly against his chest, he began to hum. The song was "I've Grown Accustomed to Her Face."

"That's one of my favorites, Tanner. Please sing it."

He smiled. "It worked for Henry Higgins; maybe it'll work for me." He released her, then led her to a chair. Kneeling, he took her hand and sang the love song.

His rich voice filled the quiet room with beautiful melody. Amanda sat very still, letting the music flow around her, in her, through her. She thought how closely music and love were intertwined, especially for the two of them. She imagined that she heard the faint echo of music from years gone by, lovely harmony that had linked her life to Tanner's.

With the last note resounding against the paneled walls, Tanner touched her face. Her cheeks were wet.

"Tears, Amanda?"

"For us. I'm crying for what might have been."

"Don't cry for us. There should be nothing except celebration for us. We've been given another chance. How often does that happen?" He pulled a handkerchief from his pocket and wiped her eyes. Smiling, he then held it to her nose. "Here. Blow."

She sniffed. "I'm no statistician. How often does that happen?"

"Only once every fifteen hundred love affairs."

"That's impressive, Tanner. How did you know that?"

"I made it up."

She chuckled. "You're terrible."

"I made you laugh, didn't I?"

"Yes. You always do."

"Good. Keep that pretty smile on your face. Let's go outside and play in the snow."

She shook her head. "Snow in the Delta. What will you think of next?"

"I'm thinking of this new position. It's called the pretzel. I saw it in a foreign film once, over in Tokyo."

"You're making that up."

"Wanna bet?"

She put her hands on her hips and grinned at him. "No. I'm from Missouri. Show me."

"Before or after the snow?"

She pretended to be in great thought, all the while watching the play of laughter on his face. That was how she would remember him, she decided. Laughing.

"After lengthy consideration I've decided to forgo the pleasures of the pretzel until after I've given you a thorough drenching in the snow. One you richly deserve, I might add."

They put on their coats and went outside to join the rest of the Donovans in the imported snow.

The snow looked as out of place as overalls at a black-tie dinner. It was heaped four inches deep on the patio. All around, the black Delta earth sprouted evergreen shrubs and holly, and even one late-blooming rose.

Paul and Martie and the twins were at the far side of the patio, building a snowman. Hallie was in the midst of a rowdy snowball fight with her teenage nieces and nephews. She let fly a snowball that caught Tanner squarely on the chest as he and Amanda stepped through the door.

"Look who's come to join the fight. Slowpoke!" Hallie yelled.

"Let's give them a run for their money, Amanda." Taking her hand, he ducked behind a redwood picnic table and began preparing his ammunition.

The fight was on—Tanner and Amanda against Hallie and her troops. Snowballs zinged through the air, melting in the warm Delta sun almost as soon as they found their mark.

"We have the advantage, Mandy," Tanner told her. "Keep low, behind the table. They'll never roust us out."

"We've got them on the run." Hallie moved in closer. "Come out from behind that table and fight like a man, Tanner."

Tanner could never resist a challenge, and Amanda knew it. She cheered as he gave a war whoop and bolted around the table. He caught Hallie in a flying tackle and rolled her in the snow.

"How's that, smarty pants?"

"Reinforcements," Hallie yelled. "Where are you when I need you?"

The nieces and nephews were also cheering for Tanner.

"Get her, Uncle Tanner. She ate the last piece of gingerbread," Theo's oldest called.

"Yeah, and her dogs chewed up my football," Theo's youngest said.

"Traitors." Hallie pounded Tanner's chest. "Let me up, you big bear, or I'll have Roseann turn the dogs loose."

Tanner grinned up at Charles's sixteen-year-old daughter. "You wouldn't, would you?"

"I'd consider it. We women have to stick together."

"Truce." Tanner released Hallie and stood up, holding his hands above his head.

A snowball caught him squarely in the face. He turned to discover the culprit. Amanda had her hand cocked back, ready to release another.

"What is this? A petticoat conspiracy?"

"Yes. Ready, women . . . aim and fire." At her signal Tanner's nieces bombarded him with snowballs.

"Amanda, I'll get you for this." She took refuge behind the picnic table as he stalked her, pelting him with soggy snowballs hastily made from the rapidly melting snow.

"You'll have to catch me first." Lobbing one last snowball, Amanda raced across the patio and into a stand of pine trees. Tanner came hard on her heels.

"Come on, troops, time to go caroling." They heard Hallie's command and the shouts of the Donovan clan, but they were too busy with their chase to notice.

Tanner cornered Amanda behind a pine tree. Swinging her over his shoulder, he marched to the newly deserted patio and lowered her to the snow. He pinned her beneath him, took a handful of snow, and carefully rubbed it in her face.

"Revenge is so sweet," he said.

"It's also cold. Tanner, what are the statistics on ladies dying in the snow in fifty-degree weather?" He was so busy enjoying his triumph, he didn't see her reach out and clutch a handful of snow.

"Never, if they have a gentleman to keep them warm." He circled her lips with his tongue, then raised back up to look at her laughing face.

"A pity you're no gentleman." In one swift move she reached up and dropped snow down the back of his shirt.

"Remember what happened the last time you did that, Mandy?"

"No," she said, lying. She remembered it very well.

"You had to go to great lengths to get me warm again." He stood up, taking her with him. "Nostalgia has an appeal at Christmastime, don't you think?"

"Yes," she said softly. She had to touch him, to feel the solidness of flesh and bone that told her he was really there beside her. Reaching out, she traced his fine cheekbones and the firm, square line of his jaw. "So long ago, Tanner." Her fingers played over his lips, memorizing them for the lonesome days when he would no longer be hers. "The house was empty then."

"It is now." He pulled her into his arms. "The entire family has gone caroling."

She rubbed her cheek against his, reveling in the feel of him, marveling at the way her love for him kept growing. "Aren't we going?"

"We'll catch up to them later." He lifted her into his arms and started up the back steps. "That is, if you want to."

The door popped shut behind them, and they were all alone in the Donovan house. There was no sound except Tanner's footsteps on the polished wooden floors, and yet Amanda seemed to hear the echoes of love and laughter within the walls of the old house.

Tanner's progress toward the bedroom was slow, for he had to keep stopping to revive himself with a kiss from Amanda. She was more than happy to oblige.

At the top of the stairs he set her on her feet and claimed another lengthy kiss. "Hmm, you're better than a St. Bernard at rescuing men who are frozen stiff."

Her hand played along the front of his pants. "If that's frozen, I hope it never thaws."

Tanner smiled. "How did you get to be so shy?"

"Practice."

"Come here, you." He pulled her into his bedroom and began to strip off her clothes. "I have in mind another kind of practice."

He took his time, unveiling her more than undressing her. Each time he saw her body, he marveled anew at its perfection. There was some unexpected delight under every garment he removed.

Her bra, damp from the snow, joined her blouse on the thick carpet.

"I never noticed that tiny scar." His voice was thick with passion as he reached out and touched the side of her breast.

"From chicken pox."

He wet the scar with his tongue. "Let me kiss it and make it well." Hungrily he moved toward her nipple. It was peaked and ready for his mouth.

She arched against him. "Tanner," she whispered, "how can I ever let you go?"

He couldn't reply, for he was feasting on her with greedy urgency. His hands moved down to her waist, expert now at opening her zipper with the least amount of effort. Deftly he peeled her slacks off, standing back to admire the view.

He bent down and kissed the indention of her navel, the soft down of her abdomen. "There," he murmured. "There is where our children will take life."

She almost believed him. "Tanner." His name was a breathless sigh. "Now. I want you now."

She felt herself being lifted, felt the puffy quilts against her back, felt the heavy tumescence of Tanner as he entered her. Their loving was slow and languorous, every stroke and counterthrust made achingly beautiful by their shared regard for each other.

There in the bed of his boyhood, Tanner poured his heart and soul into her. Loving this woman in this house, he thought, was almost a benediction, a blessing on the life he knew they'd have together. With his eyes gleaming down into hers, he took her simply, without frills, thrusting deeper and deeper until he felt the sudden hot clenching of her climax. Then he spilled his seed.

Afterward they lay in silence for a long time, arms and legs entwined, fingers laced together, cheeks pressed close. The moment felt almost sacred to them. Neither wanted it to end.

"I feel too good to move," Amanda said, stretching and yawning. "But I suppose we should dress. Your family will be back soon."

"Not until after dark They don't miss a single house with their caroling. It's a family tradition."

She sat up and caressed his face. "I made you miss it. I'm sorry."

"Don't be. I'm not." He circled her waist with his arms and pressed his lips to her abdomen. "My beautiful Amanda. Love of my life."

She touched his hair with her lips. "You say romantic things, Tanner."

He sat up, leaned against the headboard, and pulled her to him. "I mean every one of them. It will take me a lifetime to say everything that's in my heart."

She cupped his chin. "You're so special to me, Tanner Donovan. I love you."

"Then marry me."

She turned her face from him. "It's Christmas Eve. Let's not spoil it."

"All right." He got out of bed whistling. She was almost disappointed that he didn't argue. Sometimes she didn't understand herself.

"Your clothes are wet. I'll find something of Hallie's for you to wear."

"Good. And then do you think we might catch up with your family? I suddenly have the urge to go caroling."

He grinned at her. "I make you feel like singing?"

"You can take the credit if you want to."

"Then I will."

Amanda got into the shower while Tanner found her some clothes. Then he came in to scrub her back and ended up in the shower with her.

By the time they were dressed, twilight had descended on the Delta. Tanner saddled Napoleon, and he and Amanda set off to find the Donovan carolers.

They caught up with the rest of the clan at the Swanson farm. The entire Swanson family was on the front porch listening to the wagonload of Donovans sing. Tanner eased Napoleon to a halt behind the wagon. His parents swiveled their heads around when he and Amanda joined in to sing the beautiful old song, "What Child Is This?" Anna smiled a secret smile.

Tanner slept late on Christmas morning. Amanda leaned over him and felt his brow. Nothing short of sickness, she thought, would keep him from his early-morning jog. He stirred slightly under her touch, his brow cool and moist, a smile on his lips.

She slipped from the bed, dressed quietly, and went downstairs. Yesterday's mail was still on the table, untouched. She flipped through the letters, noting the usual bills and Christmas cards.

It was the last envelope that caught her attention. Addressed to Miss Amanda Lassiter in a handwriting all too familiar to her, it stood out from the rest. Claude. Why would she hear from him after six years? Her hand shook as she opened the envelope. Inside was a Christmas card, no note, no message, simply the usual Merry Christmas and Happy New Year greeting and his signature—Love, Claude.

She shivered. The card was an invasion. With Tanner upstairs in bed, just looking at the signature felt like a betrayal.

"Why, Claude?" she whispered. "Why now?"

She heard Tanner's whistling before she saw him. Quickly she put the mail back on the table and stuffed Claude's card under the bottom of the stack.

Tanner came into view, dressed in long white beard, red stocking cap, and boxer shorts.

"Ho, Ho, Ho. Mer-ry Christ-mas."

She burst into laughter. "Doesn't it get a little breezy at the North Pole in that outfit, Santa?"

"Mrs. Claus keeps me warm." He swung her up for a resounding kiss. "Are you jealous?"

"Extremely. I don't want you fooling around at the North Pole with anybody else."

"Speaking of poles . . ." He set her on her feet and pressed his hips against hers.

"We must do something about that condition, Santa," she murmured.

And they did—under the Christmas tree with the blinking lights making patterns of red and green and gold on their bare skin.

Afterward they exchanged gifts. For once Tanner had agreed to keep it simple. Hers was a simple gold bracelet, engraved with the date. His was a pair of silver spurs, to complete his courting outfit, she told him.

Claude's card was completely forgotten as they made a huge brunch and ate it at Aunt Emma's rosewood table.

Knowing that the next day Amanda would go back to work and their time together would be limited, they tried to cram as much into Christmas Day as they could. They carried gifts to Amanda's neighbors, visited the Donovans long enough for Christmas hugs and Christmas turkey, then loaded Napoleon into the horse van and set off for the river.

They arrived in time to see the sunset over the water.

"What a beautiful way to end a day," Tanner said.

"What a beautiful way to end anything."

"Amanda . . ."

"You'll be leaving in a week, Tanner. We might as well face that."

"Not without you. I want you in Dallas with me. As my wife."

"I'm tempted, Tanner. I'm so tempted."

"Then what's holding you back?"

The Christmas card slipped into her mind, a stark reminder that the past would always be with them.

"The past, Tanner. You say you've forgotten it . . ."

"I have."

"But I'm afraid we've simply shut the door on it. It's there, waiting to jump out at us. I failed at one marriage—partially, I think, because I could never forget you. I won't go into another marriage dragging the past with me."

"Hellfire and damnation, Amanda." Tanner jumped up and began to pace alongside the river. "If I could see Claude right now, I'd thrash him. Damnit all, Mandy. I love you!"

"And I love you—just as I did more than eleven years ago."

She saw the barely controlled fury in his face, watched him reign it in. Suddenly he lifted her into the saddle.

"Let's ride."

And they did. They raced along the river as if they were trying to outrun the demons that pursued them. Napoleon's hooves pounded the ground as the knowledge of their inevitable separation pounded into their hearts.

When the ride was over, they returned Napoleon to the barn and sought to push away reality with their lovemaking. Desperate to forget, their joining became almost a battle in the hay. Amanda

straddled him as Tanner panted beneath her. In
one swift, fluid movement he became dominant,
lifting her hips to his and plunging into her while
the rafters rang with their urgent cries of love.

Beneath them, Napoleon whinnied and pawed
the stable floor. He didn't know that the distur-
bance in the barn was the futile attempt of two
people to wipe out the past.

For the next two days Amanda was jumpy, her
nerves stretched tight, and she was tired. Spending her days at the shop and her nights with
Tanner, trying to make every minute count, she
felt as if she'd become frayed at the edges.

Maxine, never one to hold her tongue, felt obliged
to offer advice. "For Pete's sake, Amanda. When
are you going to stop this foolishness and say yes
to the man?"

"It's not that simple, and you know it," Amanda
said, snapping at her friend, something she rarely
did. She felt an immediate twinge of regret. "I'm
sorry. I have no right to take out my problems on
you."

"Shout, yell, scream—do anything you want to.
I'm thick-skinned. Besides, I'm your best friend."
She came and put her arms around Amanda's
shoulders. "Take my advice and face whatever is
bothering you."

Maxine didn't press for a reply; she continued
her work in the shop, doing her cheerful best to
dispel Amanda's gloom.

A winter gale developed in mid-afternoon. The
shrieking wind and thrashing rain matched Amanda's mood. She felt bleak inside, and the urge to
rage against fate was so great that she had a hard
time containing it.

"There's no need to keep the shop open," she

told Maxine. "Nobody will come out in this storm. Besides that, I'm sick of smiling when I don't feel like it."

"There's a cure for that, you know."

"If you tell me it's Tanner, I'm going to scream."

"For once in my life I'm not going to be flippant." She put on her coat and began to button it. "Tanner probably is the cure, Amanda. At least it appears to me that the man really loves you. But the only way to chase the blues is to search your heart and mind until you find the cause— then *do something about it!*" She fastened the last button on her coat and grabbed her purse. "There. I've had my say. I feel just like Dear Abby."

Amanda hugged her neck. "You look just like dear Maxine. Thank you."

"Don't mention it. Just put it in the form of a bonus check."

Both of them were laughing when Maxine left the shop. Amanda stood at the window until she saw her friend get into her old Ford and drive off, then she turned back to close up. To help chase her blues, she turned on the radio. The station was playing Glenn Miller songs. Picking up a red satin gown one of her customers had dropped across the back of a chair, Amanda waltzed across the floor. Pretending to be gay and carefree made her feel better.

She held the gown at arm's length. "My dear, you look lovely in red. May I have this next dance?"

"Certainly, you devastating thing," she said, answering her own question.

Alternately chuckling and humming, she waltzed on toward the clothes rack. Behind her, the shop bell tinkled.

She whirled around, her cheeks almost as bright as the dress. Tanner stood in the doorway, dripping all over the floor. Such love flowed through her, she thought she would faint with the intensity. She stood facing him, clutching the dress to her chest, and suddenly she knew that she could never let him go. Whatever had happened in the past, whatever was between them now, had to be resolved. Some wonderful twist of fate had brought them together again, and she had been blind to think she could ever part from him.

Without saying a word, Tanner closed and locked the door. His eyes were bright with purpose as he stalked her. When he was close enough to touch, he reached out and removed the dress from her hands.

"May I cut in?"

"Always." She went into his arms. The sounds of rain and the Glenn Miller Orchestra invaded the shop as they waltzed.

"We fit together so well," Tanner said.

"Yes. As if we were made for each other."

"We were."

"I agree. It would be a shame for us to part."

"A sin."

She sighed against his shoulder. "I suggest we make this arrangement permanent."

His arms tightened, but he kept on dancing. "Is this a proposal?"

"Yes."

"You're asking me to marry you?" She could hear the exultation in his voice.

"Yes."

"I know a preacher."

"Shall we call him?"

"Not unless you want him to be a part of this victory celebration." He waltzed her into the lounge at the back of the shop without missing a beat.

"What celebration?"

He stopped dancing and gazed down at her in

that long, languid look of absolute possession and unadulterated desire she'd come to know well.

"This one." He undressed her with reverence and care, then stood back in admiration. "I will cherish you forever." Reaching out, he ever so gently traced her cheekbones. "That face has never been far from my mind, not in all these years."

She stood very still, scarcely daring to breathe. She didn't want a thing to mar this precious moment. Today she was entrusting herself to the man she loved. She was making a commitment, and there would be no going back.

His hands moved down the side of her throat, across her shoulders, and back to her breasts. Holding them in his hands like precious gifts, he bent down and kissed their pointed tips. New life tingled through her. She felt wonderfully vibrant, gloriously happy. Her hands smoothed his dark hair. It was a gesture of tenderness, comfort, and reassurance.

"You are a special man, Tanner Donovan. I love you, and nothing will ever change that."

"And you are a special woman—my woman. Nothing will ever change *that*." He looked deep into her eyes. "That's a promise, Mandy."

Their lips met tenderly, softly, sealing the vows they'd made. As always with them, their passion was explosive. The sweet kiss quickly escalated. Tanner crushed her close, bending her body under his so he could thoroughly claim her mouth. Their moans were lost in the raging of the storm against the shop windows.

"You're wearing too many clothes, Tanner." Amanda's hands were eager, tearing aside his shirt so that buttons flew all over the room. He helped her by flinging aside his shirt and shoving off his pants. His belt buckle clanged against the floor.

Lifting her hips to his, he entered her standing up, as a boom of thunder rattled the shop.

She was flushed, filled with love, joy, and Tanner. "You certainly know how to make an entrance."

"Wait until you see the performance."

He treated her to a glorious love waltz around the room. The frenzy of their lovemaking kept pace with the frenzy of the storm. Tanner's waltz became a frantic jazz number. Not a single prop went unused. With the table under her hips and the rain battering the shop, she knew the full force of him. He eased into a fox-trot as he moved them, still joined, to the sofa. Outside, the winds roared and moaned, and lightning split the sky. Tanner and Amanda matched the storm, mood for mood.

When the sofa became too confining, they rolled to the floor. The storm released its final fury, pounding relentlessly and flooding the streets with water. Tanner imitated the storm. Under him, Amanda was damp and limp and sated.

He gently lifted her back onto the sofa. Holding her in her arms, he caressed her.

"I came to the shop to rescue you from the storm."

She smiled. "It seems you brought it inside."

He kissed the top of her head. "Are you cold?"

"No, but keep holding me. Don't ever let go."

"I don't intend to. That's another reason I came to the shop. Today while I was at home waiting for you, I realized that you had been right all along."

"Right about what?"

"The past still being between us. I can't let you go; I *won't* let you go. But I believe the only way to keep you is to face Claude."

"I'm scared." She squeezed her arms around his chest. "You're right. It's the only way. I've known it for a long time and simply didn't want to face it. Today I was miserable knowing I had chosen the coward's way out. Oh, Lord, Tanner." She buried her face in his neck. "I was going to let you go rather than face the past."

"But you didn't."

"No. When I saw you standing in the doorway, I knew I had to have you. Forever."

He eased her out of his arms far enough so that he could look into her eyes.

"Everything will be all right, Amanda. We'll make it work."

Nine

They decided to drive to Fulton, Missouri.

Amanda made arrangements for her Christmas clerks to come in and help Maxine with the shop, and Tanner talked with his business manager in Dallas. Because Tanner was so frequently out of town making personal appearances, his corporations were set up to operate with a minimum of his attention. Business matters ran smoothly for them.

It was the personal matters that got out of hand. Both of them dreaded the confrontation with Claude, and they had vastly different ideas about how to handle the situation.

The night of the storm, Amanda and Tanner were in the kitchen discussing their plans. She stood at the chopping block dicing vegetables to stir-fry while he worked at the sink washing spinach for a salad. Rain still peppered against the windows.

"I think we should call him." Amanda's knife lopped off the head of a fat carrot. "Let him know we're coming."

"No. He might tell us not to come." Tanner

ripped into the spinach. "We *have* to see him in person in order to get all this out into the open."

"What if he's not there?" Her knife clicked rapidly against the chopping block. Severed vegetables rolled away as if in fright.

"Doesn't he run a newspaper?" Tanner attacked the spinach as if it were a threat to world peace.

"Yes, but . . ."

"Dammit all, Amanda, if he's not in Fulton, we'll find him."

"How?" She brandished a carrot stick in the air. "Wave a magic wand?"

Tanner reigned in his temper. He'd come too far to let a foolish argument over Claude spoil everything. "Businessmen simply can't disappear," he said more calmly. "Their secretaries always know where to find them."

Amanda abandoned her vegetables and flung her arms around him. "I don't know why I'm letting a little thing like this get me so upset. I'm sorry, Tanner."

"That's a relief. For a minute there I thought you were going to beat me with that carrot stick."

She laughed, squeezing him harder. "You won't let anything happen to us, will you?"

"Never. We've come this far. Only a few more hurdles to go and we'll be walking down the aisle and living happily ever after."

Amanda went back to her chopping block. "Tanner, do you think we can live happily ever after on this?" She held up the pitiful remains of the vegetables. They weren't diced; they were mutilated. "I suppose we'll have to depend on your salad tonight."

He grinned sheepishly. "This poor stuff?" He held up shred of spinach no bigger than a toothpick. "I guess I got carried away."

"Maybe I have some olives and cheese in the refrigerator."

"I need something more substantial for the task ahead."

"Facing Claude?"

"No. Kissing and making up."

They made quick use of Aunt Emma's rosewood table and ended up eating at Doe's.

Later that night Tanner lay in bed staring at the ceiling. He was remembering Claude.

When they were six, they'd started school together. By the second week they were fast friends. It was an unlikely friendship: Tanner was big and brash and outgoing; Claude was small and studious and quiet. A frog was what brought them together. Tanner had caught the biggest bullfrog in his pond and brought it to school in his lunch pail. His intention was to take bets at recess on how far the frog could jump. He had his eye on a red wagon in Tudberry's window. He could imagine himself sauntering up to Tudberry's after school, his pockets full of money, buying the wagon. He knew just how it would feel when he whizzed down the hill in back of his barn in that new wagon.

But the frog had other ideas. Around midmorning it pushed open the lunch box lid and hopped out to investigate its new surroundings. Unfortunately it chose to investigate the underside of Miss Margaret Riley's dress. When the teacher started screaming, nobody knew what it was all about except Tanner and Claude. Both of them had seen the frog leave the safety of the lunch pail.

The frog soon made itself known. Finding nothing exciting in Miss Riley's bloomers—at least, that's the way Claude later told the story—it hopped onto her desk. Fifteen little boys and ten little girls gave merry chase. It was Claude who helped Tanner corner the frog.

"Is this yours?" he'd whispered.

"Yeah."

"Golly. He's a whopper."

"You won't tell, will you? Miss Riley will wear my britches out."

"Naw."

When Miss Riley had recovered enough to question her pupils about the frog, Claude had stepped forward and told the biggest tale Tanner had ever heard. "I saw that big ol' frog this morning down beside that little pond behind the schoolhouse. Seems to me it looked mighty bored. Matter of fact, it got interested in my reader and followed me to school. I saw it come creeping through our door a little while ago. Miss Riley, I guess that ol' frog wanted to learn how to read."

Miss Riley had been so enchanted, she'd forgotten about punishment. After that Claude and Tanner had been best friends. Tanner was the school hero, and Claude was the school storyteller. They'd made quite a team.

Later they'd both fallen in love with Amanda. It seemed that both of them noticed her at the same time. Until the seventh grade she'd been just another little redheaded girl with pigtails. Suddenly she was the prettiest thing they'd ever laid eyes on—and both of them wanted to marry her. It took a fight in the dirt behind the cafeteria to settle the matter. Claude had ended up with a bloody nose, and Tanner had ended up with a black eye—and Amanda. After that the matter was settled. Amanda was always Tanner's, and Claude was always their very best friend.

Until eleven years ago.

Tanner reached across the bed and touched Amanda, just to reassure himself. She was there, warm and soft, hips curved under the covers, outlined by the moonlight. Quietly he rose from the bed.

At times like this he almost wished he smoked. He looked at the bedside clock. Two A.M. The next day they'd be leaving for Missouri—a two-day drive. He needed his rest. But memories of Claude beat through his mind. The hammer blows wrecked his peace and destroyed any chance of sleep.

Dressing quickly in a sweat suit and jogging shoes, he eased out the door and down the stairs. He would run until he could regain some semblance of tranquillity.

Then he'd be ready to face Claude.

Amanda woke with a start.

She'd been dreaming that Claude wanted to marry her again. She kept seeing him over and over, arms outstretched, calling to her—love, love, love. She sat up and brushed her hair back from her face.

"Tanner?"

Turning, she saw the empty spot where he had been. Panic seized her. Oh, no! she thought. Maybe it wasn't a dream. Maybe Claude *had* come for her, and Tanner was gone again.

Her feet hit the floor running. Without even bothering to cover her nakedness, she raced down the stairs. "Tanner?" If he was anywhere in the house, he would hear her. She was yelling loud enough to alert the fire department all the way across town.

She flicked on lights as she ran. By the time she got to the kitchen, she was fully awake and feeling rather foolish. She'd been dreaming, and Tanner would never leave her. Hoping she hadn't awakened the neighbors, she went back upstairs, turning off the lights behind her. With her sanity restored, she surveyed her bedroom. Tanner's sweat suit and shoes were missing. She should have known. He always ran when he was disturbed, and certainly the prospect of facing Claude was disturbing—to both of them.

She put on her robe and walked to the window. The streets were dark and empty. Pressing her face against the windowpane, she whispered, "Go with God, Tanner."

Going back to bed was useless. She walked to her dressing table and sat down. All her Christmas cards had been tucked into the top drawer. She reached inside and took out Claude's card. "Love, Claude," it said. She pressed her fingers against the signature. Memories flooded through her.

The night of their senior prom, Tanner's old Chevrolet had died six miles from the school gymnasium. Tanner had said it wasn't too far to walk, and she had protested that she'd never make it in her high heels. Besides that, it started raining, not a gentle spring rain but an angry flood from the heavens. Just when they had resigned themselves to spending their prom night stranded in the car, Claude had come along. He'd bundled them into the backseat of his reliable Ford, and the three of them had gone to the prom together. When Tanner asked why he had no date, he'd replied, "Why do I need a date? I have my two best friends. Anyhow, I'm too busy being your guardian angel to date."

Claude had always been their guardian angel, transporting Amanda back and forth to Alabama to visit Tanner, watching over their romance with friendly benevolence, giving them moral support. Exactly when that relationship had changed, she didn't know. The change had been subtle and completely unexpected.

She smoothed the card. There could be no going back. Claude would never be their guardian angel again.

"Mandy?"

Tanner was standing in the doorway. She hadn't heard him come in.

"I couldn't sleep." She made no attempt to cover the card. From the time they'd made their commitment, she knew there could never be anything except honesty between them.

"Neither could I." He came to her and put his hand on her shoulder. The signature on the card seemed to leap out at him.

She watched as he picked it up. He stood motionless, saying nothing. His hand tightened on her shoulder. The silence echoed with all the things they might have said. Finally he placed the card carefully back on the dressing table, signature up. His fingers bit into her flesh, but still he remained silent.

She spoke first. "At the time it didn't seem necessary to tell you."

"The card said love."

"I know." She reached up and squeezed his hand. "I don't know what that means. This is the first time I've heard from Claude since the divorce."

"He wants you back. Any man in his right mind would."

She stood up and came into his arms. Pressing her cheek against his chest, she could hear the steady thrum of his heartbeat. Somehow it was reassuring to her. She'd always felt protected in Tanner's arms.

"Let's not make mountains, Tanner."

"If I take you back to Fulton, I'll be delivering you to him."

She reached up and cupped his face. "Tanner Donovan, do you doubt my love for you?"

"No."

"Do you doubt your love for me?"

"Never." His grin was apologetic.

"Then nothing can come between us. Ever. We'll face this together."

He laughed exultantly as he picked her up and carried her to the bed. "Sometimes I get the blues, Amanda. The blues can make a man crazy."

With the mattress pressing against her back and Tanner pressing against her thighs, she smiled. "I know a cure."

He swept aside her robe. "That's the best offer I've had today."

Amanda began curing his blues.

They left for Missouri at six o'clock the next morning. Both of them were groggy from lack of sleep but determined to be cheerful.

Tanner dragged out his repertoire of old football jokes and regaled Amanda all the way to Memphis. She laughed at the first twenty or so, but finally she could stand it no more.

"Tanner, if you tell me another football story, I'm going to turn blue in the face and faint and bash my head on the door handle and bleed all over the car, and we'll never get to Fulton—let alone to the altar."

He chuckled. "You laughed."

"That was hysteria, not laughter." She leaned her weary head against the back of the seat. "I may break out in hives. Why did we decide to drive instead of fly?"

"I think it was your idea."

"No. I believe it was yours."

"Are we quarreling again, Amanda?"

"Yes. If I weren't so tired, I'd come over there and make up."

"On the interstate?"

She shrugged her shoulders. "What can I say? I'm a wicked woman."

She gave him a tired smile, closed her eyes, and fell fast asleep. She slept all the way to Little Rock. Then Tanner let her drive.

They decided to spend the night at Cape Girardeau. They were both anxious and out of sorts.

"What if Claude is hostile when he sees us?" Amanda asked over the dinner table.

"Claude has never been hostile. That's not his nature."

"Are you defending him?"

"He was my best friend."

"He was my husband."

They glared at each other over their tough pork chops.

"If I discover Claude ever laid a hand on you, I'll—"

"He never touched me. As a matter of fact, he was very good to me."

"Amanda, you're being totally irrational."

"You're just mad because I nearly wrecked the car."

"That was my fault. I never should have let you drive. You were too tired."

Big fat tears welled in her eyes and rolled down her cheeks. "Tanner, I don't want to lose you. This trip is making me crazy. Let's turn around and go home."

He came around the table so fast, the dishes rattled. "I can't stand to see you cry." He pressed his cheek to hers, then quickly took care of the bill and escorted her to their room.

Then he comforted her.

• • •

They arrived in Fulton the next afternoon at five. A light snow had fallen, and the small town looked like it belonged in a Currier and Ives print. They drove past the campuses of William Woods and Westminster, which were still deserted for the holidays, and into the downtown area.

Claude's office was in an old brick building, painted white. THE DAILY BUGLE was lettered on the north side of the building.

"This is it, Amanda." Tanner parked his car in a vacant spot and turned to face her. "Nervous?"

"Yes." She sat very straight, hands pressed together in her lap. "We had an easy divorce. Both of us knew it was time to end the marriage. But seeing him again is going to be hard."

Tanner reached over and squeezed her hands. "For me too. The last time I saw Claude, I was trying to steal you away from him at the altar. I wouldn't blame him if he took a punch at me."

They sat for a few minutes, both dreading the confrontation and postponing it as long as possible.

"It's late," Amanda said. "Maybe he's not there."

"There's only one way to find out." Tanner got out of the car and opened her door. Together they walked into the office.

Claude was alone, sitting at his desk, newspaper copy spread out in front of him. He looked up when the bell above his door tinkled. The silence was so thick, it could have been spread on toast and eaten for breakfast.

Tanner and Amanda stood inside the door, and Claude sat riveted to his chair. If thoughts had been birds, the air would have been heavy with the flapping of wings. Amanda thought Claude had aged. Tanner marveled that he felt no sudden surge of anger toward Claude, just a sad sort of ache for the things they'd lost—the easy camaraderie, the crazy jokes that nobody else thought were funny, the laughter.

The silence became embarrassing. Finally Amanda spoke.

"I received your Christmas card, Claude."

"Good. I meant what I said."

Amanda felt Tanner's body tense. She slipped her arm around his waist and squeezed.

Claude took off his glasses and polished the lenses with his handkerchief, a habit that signaled his unease. Tanner and Amanda watched him silently, remembering the many times they'd seen him do exactly the same thing.

Finally Claude put the glasses firmly back on his nose. "I've always loved you, Amanda," he said simply.

"Amanda is going to marry *me*, Claude." Tanner hadn't meant to blurt out the news like that, but he was going crazy being in the same room with Claude, knowing he'd once held Amanda and made love to her and kissed all her secret places. The rage he'd held in check suddenly surfaced. Visions of the two of them together clouded his judgment. He balled his fists and took a step toward Claude.

To his astonishment Claude burst out laughing. "Thank God for that. I've always known the two of you belonged together."

Tanner's rage ebbed, but his nerves were still raw from lack of sleep. "Then why in the hell did you send that card and sign it 'love'?"

"I'm a sentimental fool. I just wanted Amanda to know that there are no hard feelings." He stood up and came to her. When he was close enough, he reached for her hand. "The six years we had together were like a gift, Amanda, one I never expected to receive, and one I never fully appreciated. You've always belonged to Tanner. Deep down I knew that, even when we were married."

"I'm sorry, Claude—for everything. For coming between you and Tanner, for the divorce—"

His laughter interrupted her. "Don't say another word. The next thing I know, you'll be saying you're sorry for the marriage—one that nearly didn't take place, thanks to you." He turned to Tanner. "That was a helluva stunt you pulled in the church."

"It was the high point of my career." Tanner was almost relaxed enough to grin but not quite. He couldn't figure out why Claude was so amiable, and he didn't trust his old friend's willingness to give up Amanda now that he had seen her again. The man had to be crazy, Tanner decided.

"Maybe I should pay you back. When is the wedding?"

It was a sticky question. Tanner didn't want Claude at his wedding. He wanted to start his marriage with a clean slate, no reminders of the past.

"We haven't set the date," Amanda said, noting the look of thanks in Tanner's eyes.

Claude clapped Tanner on the shoulder. "That doesn't sound like you. I'd have thought you'd have her kidnapped by now."

"I guess I've mellowed with old age."

"Could be." Claude rubbed his hand through his sparse hair. "We've all changed a bit." He grinned. "Not that I have any reason to complain."

This meeting wasn't at all what Tanner had expected. He'd anticipated bitterness and hostility, and he still couldn't trust the joviality Claude exhibited. He could understand artificial cheerfulness as a front to cover hurt, but somehow Claude's feelings seemed genuine.

"You're looking good, Claude. How's the newspaper?" Small talk, Tanner thought, the great conversation rescuer.

"Doing great. Remember that new section you wanted to add, Amanda? The family-life section?"

"I remember you were opposed to the idea."

"But you finally convinced me. It's the best thing that ever happened to me."

"Did it increase circulation?" Amanda didn't have her mind on circulation; she was wondering why Claude seemed so relaxed and cheerful.

"It did more than that. But I'd prefer to show you than tell you. You know my flair for the dramatic. I guess that's why I didn't write a note on the Christmas card. Have dinner with me tonight. Our—my house."

The correction stung Tanner. Claude had meant the house he'd shared with Amanda. Tanner would rather walk on a bed of nails than see the inside of that house.

Amanda sensed his reluctance and understood. She quickly intervened and made arrangements for them to meet Claude at a restaurant. There were still things that needed to be said. She and Tanner had come too far to leave without finishing what they'd started.

The two hours they spent in the motel, waiting for the appointed dinner hour, seemed like forever. Amanda fiddled with the radio until she found some decent music, then, in pretended gaiety, danced around the small room. After bouncing into Tanner four times he finally complained that he wasn't going to have any feet left, and she quit. Tanner, of course, resorted to his bad football jokes. Amanda squelched her screams of agony.

Neither of them mentioned what had happened at the newspaper office. It had gone too easily. They didn't dare voice their separate skepticism, for fear they'd put a jinx on the trip.

Finally it was time to meet Claude. He was waiting for them outside the restaurant. He looked as cheerful as before.

"I don't understand Claude anymore. You'd think

a man who'd lost the most desirable woman in the whole world would be doing something besides standing on the sidewalk smiling like a jackass eating saw briers." Uncertainty had made Tanner testy. He whipped his car into a space that appeared too small. He hated situations he didn't understand, and he'd be damned if he could figure Claude out.

"Be charitable, Tanner. I think he looks a little tired, like he's working too hard."

Amanda's wifely comment about Claude grated on Tanner's nerves. For a moment he considered backing out of the parking space and heading back to Greenville as fast as he could. But he didn't—he got out and opened Amanda's door. When she reached up and put her hand in his, he melted inside. They'd survive, he decided. This trip had to be the supreme test. They were seeing each other at their worst, and it hadn't lessened his love for Amanda one iota. He hoped she felt the same about him.

He put his arms around her waist and smiled.

"Let's go see what your ex-husband has to show us."

Claude greeted them and took them inside the restaurant to their table, all the while making small talk. He asked about their parents, Tanner's brothers and sisters, and Maxine. He inquired about changes in their hometown. He was maddenly calm, and whatever he had to show them apparently would wait. There was no mention of why they were sitting at a table for eight. There was no sign of the dramatic surprise he'd hinted at earlier. But they noticed that from time to time he looked down at his watch.

Claude ordered drinks. Tanner experienced a sense of déjà vu. When they were a threesome in the old days, Claude had been the one to place the orders. Usually he and Amanda were too engrossed in each other to pay attention to mundane things such as food and drink.

As they sipped their drinks a little boy raced through the restaurant and came to a stop beside Claude's chair. He wore red long johns, overalls with no shirt, and enough freckles to decorate at least three more boys.

"Hey, Claude. We got here late because Mama had to keep fixin' her face, but don't tell her I said so." His red cowlick bounced up and down, and his brown eyes sparkled with devilment as he scooted into a chair.

Claude beamed. "Tanner and Amanda, I'd like you to meet John."

That was all he said, simply "John." Tanner and Amanda were mystified and speechless. But that didn't matter, for John talked a mile a minute. Leaning close to Claude, he said in a conspiratorial manner that could be heard three tables away, "They're slow as molasses. Betcha ol' Mary Lou had to stop at the ladies' room and pull up her petticoat. It's always showin'. And Mama was scared her lipstick would be crooked. And Petey always wets his pants when he gets excited. 'Course, I never do. Seven's too old to wet your britches." Abruptly he turned to Amanda and grinned. "Say! You sure are pretty. You used to be Claude's wife, didn't you? That's what Mama said. She's been in a fizzle all day 'cause you was back in town." He stopped talking long enough to hitch up his overalls and prop his elbows on the table. "Say, Claude. I sure am hungry."

John didn't wait for a reply, and that was fine, since nobody could get a word in edgewise, anyway. "Look. There's Mama now." He jumped up and waved. "Hey, Mama. We're over here."

"Mama" stood in the doorway hesitantly, holding the hand of a rather damp-looking little boy who no doubt was Petey. Beside her stood a young girl, pudgy and sullen, looking as if she were entering the restaurant and puberty with equal defiance.

Claude went to the woman and led her, almost reverently, back to their table. "Helen, these are the friends I told you about." Standing with his arm around her, he turned to Amanda and Tanner. "I'd like you to meet Helen Burnaw, the woman I'm going to marry."

Tanner was astounded. The woman was at least six years older than Claude, maybe more. She was about as different from Amanda as a woman could be. Claude always had been softhearted. Tanner's first guess would have been that she was a widow, and Claude had taken the family under his wing. Or perhaps she was a friend from church or from his neighborhood.

He could sense Amanda's astonishment. Both of them spoke at the same time, uttering the usual polite greeting one gives to strangers. Then a remarkable thing happened. Helen Burnaw smiled. Tanner was flabbergasted at the transformation. The woman who was so insignificant-looking, she nearly blended into the furniture, became radiant, almost beautiful. And her voice! Hearing it was to be enchanted. It was low-pitched, breathless, and sexy. Tanner felt a surge of gladness for Claude—and a selfish sense of relief for himself.

"And this is Mary Lou and little Petey." Claude finished the introductions as he helped Helen and her children to their seats. "Helen moved to Fulton two years ago. Her husband died. She came to work for me—handling the family-living section, Amanda." He grinned proudly, as if the rest was self-explanatory.

"Congratulations Claude—and Helen." Amanda felt as if she'd gone to the movie theater expecting to see a tragedy and ended up seeing a comedy. She thought of the sleepless nights she'd spent and of her ragged nerves, and she wanted to burst into laughter. Her mother always had told her worry was a foolish emotion. She wished she'd paid more attention.

Talk among the adults was stilted and awkward at first—and possible only because John was too busy eating to interrupt. Then, when three-year-old Petey crawled under the table and squashed French fries on Tanner's shoes, they all loosened up. Tanner, who was accustomed to children, viewed the episode with kind indulgence. Besides, it gave him a chance to tell some of his favorite stories about Paul and Martie's twins.

The meal gradually drew to a close. Tanner and Amanda felt sad at its end. All of them knew that they'd passed another milestone in their relationship. They'd come full circle, from three people who were bound together by circumstances, to best friends, to enemies, and back to three people with a common bond. Amanda, who had loved them both, was the pivot. Her marriage to Claude couldn't be stricken from the books and forgotten. It would always be a part of her past. But now she could look at it as a pleasant interlude, rather than as a wall that separated her from Tanner. Knowing that Claude had let her go emotionally, freed them to love totally. Whatever angry passion had haunted the three of them could be forgiven.

Claude asked Helen to wait while he followed Tanner and Amanda to their car. On the street he shook Tanner's hand. "I'm really glad that you and Amanda are going to be married. It makes everything right. What happened can't be changed, but perhaps we're all the wiser for the experience." Turning to Amanda, he hugged her. "Be happy, sweetheart."

"You, too, Claude," she whispered. At that moment he was more dear to her than he had ever been.

"Keep in touch, Claude." Tanner slapped him on the shoulder.

"You, too, buddy."

Tanner and Amanda climbed into the car. Claude stood on the sidewalk until they were out of sight. The sadness Amanda had felt weighed heavily on her heart. She knew that keeping in touch meant sending cards at Christmas and giving occasional thought to the memories they shared. But that was life, she realized. People and circumstances changed.

Amanda brushed a tear from her eye as they rounded the street corner and Claude disappeared from view.

"Isn't this the point in the movie where violins play and the hero carries the heroine off into the sunset?"

Tanner reached for her hand. "You don't have to be brave for me, Mandy." Lifting her hand, he pressed it to his lips. "It's over. You can cry on my shoulder if you want to."

And she did. The bittersweet tears of emotional release.

Ten

During the long drive back home they made plans.

"We'll get married next week," Tanner said, "and we'll live wherever you want. Dallas would be better for me, but I could move my home office without too much trouble."

"Dallas sounds great. I'll sell my antique clothing store, and we'll wait for Hannah and Jacob to come home. Can they be here by March?"

"March! You've just broken my heart."

"Let me kiss it and make it well." She did, through his shirt. "Better?"

"Yes. There are other parts of me that could use attention."

"I promise to devote my full attention to all those other parts if you'll promise me something."

"Anything. The sun, the moon, a football team, a left-handed, French-speaking chef—you name it and it's yours."

"I want a big wedding, Tanner, the kind we would have had eleven years ago. I know it's my second time around and a big wedding may be tacky by some people's standards, but it's what I want."

He laughed. "Amanda, we've made headlines before. I promise you the biggest show in town."

The trumpets woke Amanda up. Without a trace of grogginess she bounded to her window and looked out. The entire Greenville High School marching band was assembled on her lawn, brass horns gleaming in the March sun, and polished shoes squashing her buttercups. Tanner, in tuxedo and top hat, was sitting atop Napoleon, directing the band.

Although he'd arrived from Dallas the previous day and she'd seen him at the wedding rehearsal, she felt a wondrous surge of joy, as if she were seeing him for the first time in years.

She propped her elbows on the windowsill and listened to the song, "A New Kind of Love." When it was over, Tanner turned toward her and saluted.

"Good morning, love. Happy wedding day."

She blew him a kiss. "You're not supposed to see the bride before the wedding. They say it's bad luck."

"My day doesn't start until I see you, and I don't believe in bad luck. Besides, I didn't want you to miss the parade."

"What parade?"

"The one you're in. Put on your wedding gown, love. We're leading the band through the streets of Greenville. I want everybody to share our joy."

She laughed with sheer delight. Life with Tanner would always be a parade.

"I'll need some help with the buttons," she called down.

"Be right up." Tanner started the band playing a love song, dismounted, and came into the house.

Amanda thought that the happiest sound she'd

ever heard were his footsteps on the stairs. She met him in the middle of the bedroom.

He kissed her thoroughly, then glanced at the bed. "What a shame to let it go to waste."

"But we might miss our own wedding."

"Can't have that." He gave her one last kiss. "Now, where's that wedding dress?"

She took the lovely Victorian dress she'd bought in Savannah from the closet. Tanner helped her slip into the billowing satin-and-lace creation, then turned her around to fasten all the tiny covered buttons that ran up the back.

His large hands fumbled. "That's one method of birth control—just keep the bridegroom unbuttoning the bride's dress."

Laughing, Amanda held her breath and waited. Tanner finally got all the buttons fastened. Together they went down the stairs and out the front door. He helped her up to sit sidesaddle, being careful not to damage her dress, and mounted behind her.

The marching band behind them, they set out for the center of town.

Lord Pritchard had cleared the streets for them. Music filled the air, brass instruments flashed in the sunshine, Napoleon pranced as if he knew it was a special occasion. Tanner and Amanda waved, and smiled and smiled and smiled. The huge crowd cheered and shouted good wishes as Greenville's favorite couple shared the happiest day of their lives with the entire town.

Later that day, just before sunset, Amanda stood in the dressing room of the church with her best friend, preparing for the actual ceremony.

Maxine pulled the Victorian gown over Amanda's head and began to fasten the buttons.

Amanda sucked in her breath.

Maxine struggled with the buttons at the waistline, then stopped to face Amanda.

"Amanda?"

Amanda smiled and nodded yes.

"Well, hot damn! Does Tanner know?"

"Not yet."

"He's going to be thrilled pea-turkey pink. How long have you known?"

"I wasn't sure until February. My first impulse was to call him, but I wanted to tell him in person. The brief weekends we've been together have been so hectic, the time didn't seem right. It will be his wedding present."

The faint echoes of Lohengrin's Wedding March drifted into the dressing room.

"Hurry and fasten those buttons, Maxine. I've waited eleven years for this."

Minutes later she stood at the back of the church and watched as Tanner's twin sisters, Hallie and Hannah, marched down the aisle. Maxine trailed sedately behind them. Then little Elizabeth skipped down the aisle, strewing rose petals and humming a nursery song under her breath.

At long last Amanda began her walk down the aisle to Tanner Donovan. He was waiting for her at the altar rail, flanked by his father and his brothers, his eyes shining.

They pledged their vows, and there was a collective sigh from the audience when Tanner kissed his bride. As the triumphant strains of the Wedding March filled the church, every head turned to watch the customary exit of the newlyweds.

Much to the delight of the guests, Tanner scooped up his bride and carried her down the aisle. His brother Jacob was waiting for them outside the church, along with Napoleon—and the sun.

Tanner lifted his bride into the saddle, and they rode off into a picture-book-perfect sunset.

They didn't have a private moment until Tanner's jet had touched down in New York and they were settled into their room at the Plaza.

He held out his arms. "Come here, Mrs. Donovan. I'm dying to get to know you better."

She lifted her face for his kiss. "I pledge to you a lifetime of love, Amanda Donovan." His mouth was hungry and eager on hers, and yet there was such tenderness in his touch that she almost wept with the sweetness of it.

Her face shone with the radiance of a madonna, as the kiss ended and she looked up at him. "Do you think you can manage a few antique buttons?"

He turned her around and began to unfasten buttons. "Does every dress you own have these blasted buttons?" he muttered, then added, "There's never been a dress designed that would keep me away from you." He slipped the garment from her shoulders and hugged her from behind, cupping her breasts. They were heavy in his hands. He bent his head, shifting her slightly so that he could capture one pointed tip in his mouth.

Amanda tangled her hands in his dark hair and pulled him down to her. As his mouth closed over her ripe fullness she glowed with joy and passion and her secret.

His eyes were shining when he lifted his head. "It's been so long, Mandy. I'd almost forgotten how perfect you are." He slid the dress over her hips, taking her slip and panties with it.

Amanda unbuttoned his shirt and ran her hands over his chest. "And I, you."

Tanner picked her up and carried her to the bed. The moonlight set off flaming highlights in her hair and touched her body with silver. Tanner knelt beside her, tracing her with his eyes and his hands.

"You've never looked more beautiful." He tenderly touched breasts, her abdomen. It curved gently under his hands. "You've been eating right, Mandy. I approve. Who's responsible? Maxine?"

"You." She smiled.

"Me?"

"Yes. Christmas Eve, I think. In your bed."

She watched as the slow dawning of comprehension and a look of joy spread across his face. Then, cocky, arrogant Tanner Donovan, who made all of life his private parade, developed tears in his eyes.

"We're going to have a baby?"

She laughed. "You don't have to whisper, Tanner. There's nobody to hear except you and me."

He pulled her into his arms and rocked her jubilantly on the bed. "I want the whole world to know. I want to lean out the window and shout it in Central Park. I want to have a parade down Fifth Avenue. I want—"

"Tanner," she said, interrupting him.

His grin was sheepish as he pulled back and looked at her. "What?"

"Do you think the parade can wait till tomorrow?"

His smile became wicked. "Do you have something else in mind, Mrs. Donovan?"

"A proper wedding night, Mr. Donovan."

He lowered her to the bed and gave her one.

THE EDITOR'S CORNER

A critic once wrote that LOVESWEPT books have "the most off-the-wall titles" of any romance line. And recently, I got a letter from a reader asking me who is responsible for the "unusual titles" of our books. (Our fans are so polite; I'll bet she wanted to substitute "strange" for unusual!) Whether off-the-wall or unusual—I prefer to think of them as memorable—our titles are dreamed up by authors as well as editors. (We editors must take the responsibility for the most outrageous titles, though.) Next month you can look forward to six wonderful LOVESWEPTs that are as original, strong, amusing—yes, even as off-the-wall—as their titles.

First, **McKNIGHT IN SHINING ARMOR,** LOVESWEPT #276, by Tami Hoag, is an utterly heartwarming story of a young divorced woman, Kelsie Connors, who has two children to raise while holding down two *very* unusual jobs. She's trying to be the complete Superwoman when she meets hero Alec McKnight. Their first encounter, while hilarious, holds the potential for disaster . . . as black lace lingerie flies through the air of the conservative advertising executive's office. But Alec is enchanted, not enraged—and then Kelsie has to wonder if the "disaster" isn't what he's done to her heart. A joyous reading experience.

SHOWDOWN AT LIZARD ROCK, LOVESWEPT #277, by Sandra Chastain, features one of the most gorgeous and exciting pairs of lovers ever. Kaylyn Smith has the body of Wonder Woman and the face of Helen of Troy, and handsome hunk King Vandergriff realizes the

(continued)

moment he sets eyes on her that he's met his match. She is standing on top of Lizard Rock, protesting his construction company's building of a private club on the town's landmark. King just climbs right up there and carries her down . . . but she doesn't surrender. (Well, not immediately.) You'll delight in the feisty shenanigans of this marvelous couple.

CALIFORNIA ROYALE, LOVESWEPT #278, by Deborah Smith, is one of the most heart-stoppingly beautiful of love stories. Shea Somerton is elegant and glamorous just like the resort she runs; Duke Araiza is sexy and fast just like the Thoroughbreds he raises and trains. Both have heartbreaking pain in their pasts. And each has the fire and the understanding that the other needs. But their goals put them at cross-purposes, and neither of them can bend . . . until a shadow from Shea's early days falls over their lives. A thrilling romance.

Get out the box of tissues when you settle down to enjoy **WINTER'S DAUGHTER,** LOVESWEPT #279, by Kathleen Creighton, because you're bound to get a good laugh and a good cry from this marvelous love story. Tannis Winter, disguised as a bag-lady, has gone out onto the streets to learn about the plight of the homeless and to search for cures for their ills. But so has town councilman Dillon James, a "derelict" with mysterious attractions for the unknowing Tannis. Dillon is instantly bewitched by her courage and compassion . . . by the scent of summer on her skin and the brilliance of winter in her eyes. Their hunger for each other grows quickly . . . and to ravenous proportions. Only a risky confrontation can clear up the misunderstandings they face, so that they can finally have it all. We think you're going to treasure this very rich and very dramatic love story.

Completing the celebration of her fifth year as a published writer, the originator of continuing character romances, Iris Johansen, gives us the breathlessly emotional love story of the Sheik you met this month, exciting Damon El Karim, in **STRONG, HOT WINDS,** LOVESWEPT #280. Damon has vowed to punish the lovely Cory Brandel, the mother of his son, whom she's kept secret from him. To do so, he has her kidnapped with the

(continued)

boy and brought to Kasmara. But in his desert palace, as they set each other off, his sense of barbaric justice and her fury at his betrayal quickly turn into quite different emotions. Bewildered by the tenderness and the wild need he feels for her, Damon fears he can never have Cory's love. But at last, Cory has begun to understand what makes this complex and charismatic man tick—and she fears she isn't strong enough to give him the enduring love he so much deserves! Crème de la crème from Iris Johansen. I'm sure you join all of us at Bantam in wishing her not five, but *fifty* more years of creating great love stories!

Closing out the month in a very big way is **PARADISE CAFE,** LOVESWEPT #281, by Adrienne Staff. And what a magnificent tale this is. Beautiful Abby Clarke is rescued by ruggedly handsome outdoorsman Jack Gallagher—a man of few words and fast moves, especially when trying to haul in the lady whom destiny has put in his path. But Abby is not a risk taker. She's an earnest, hardworking young woman who's always put her family first . . . but Jack is an impossible man to walk away from with his sweet, wild passion that makes her yearn to forget about being safe. And Jack is definitely *not* safe for Abby . . . he's a man with wandering feet. You'll relish the way the stay-at-home and the vagabond find that each has a home in the center of the other's heart. A true delight.

I trust that you'll agree with me that the six LOVE-SWEPTs next month are as memorable as their off-the-wall titles!

Enjoy!

Carolyn Nichols

Carolyn Nichols
   Editor
LOVESWEPT
Bantam Books
666 Fifth Avenue
New York, NY 10103

THE HOMETOWN HUNK CONTEST

FOR EVERY WOMAN WHO HAS EVER SAID—
"I know a man who looks
just like the hero of this book"
—HAVE WE GOT A CONTEST FOR YOU!

To help celebrate our fifth year of publishing LOVESWEPT
we are having a fabulous, fun-filled event called THE
HOMETOWN HUNK contest. We are going to reissue six
classic early titles by six of your favorite authors.

DARLING OBSTACLES by Barbara Boswell
IN A CLASS BY ITSELF by Sandra Brown
C.J.'S FATE by Kay Hooper
THE LADY AND THE UNICORN by Iris Johansen
CHARADE by Joan Elliott Pickart
FOR THE LOVE OF SAMI by Fayrene Preston

Here, as in the backs of all July, August, and September
1988 LOVESWEPTS you will find "cover notes" just like the
ones we prepare at Bantam as the background for our art
director to create our covers. These notes will describe the
hero and heroine, give a teaser on the plot, and suggest a
scene for the cover. Your part in the contest will be to see
if a great looking local man—or men, if your hometown is
so blessed—fits our description of one of the heroes of the
six books we will reissue.

   THE HOMETOWN HUNK who is selected (one for each of
the six titles) will be flown to New York via United Airlines
and will stay at the Loews Summit Hotel—the ideal hotel
for business or pleasure in midtown Manhattan—for two
nights. All travel arrangements made by Reliable Travel
International, Incorporated. He will be the model for the
new cover of the book which will be released in mid-1989.
The six people who send in the winning photos of their
HOMETOWN HUNK will receive a pre-selected assortment
of LOVESWEPT books free for one year. Please see the
Official Rules above the Official Entry Form for full details
and restrictions.

We can't wait to start judging those pictures! Oh, and you must let the man you've chosen know that you're entering him in the contest. After all, if he wins he'll have to come to New York.

Have fun. Here's your chance to get the cover-lover of your dreams!

Carolyn Nichols

Carolyn Nichols
Editor
LOVESWEPT
Bantam Books
666 Fifth Avenue
New York, NY 10102–0023

THE HOMETOWN HUNK CONTEST

DARLING OBSTACLES
(Originally Published as LOVESWEPT #95)
By Barbara Boswell

COVER NOTES

The Characters:

Hero:
GREG WILDER's gorgeous body and "to-die-for" good looks
haven't hurt him in the dating department, but when
most women discover he's a widower with four kids, they
head for the hills! Greg has the hard, muscular build of an
athlete, and his light brown hair, which he wears neatly
parted on the side, is streaked blond by the sun. Add to
that his aquamarine blue eyes that sparkle when he laughs,
and his sensual mouth and generous lower lip, and you're
probably wondering what woman in her right mind
wouldn't want Greg's strong, capable surgeon's hands working their magic on her—kids or no kids!

Personality Traits:
An acclaimed neurosurgeon, Greg Wilder is a celebrity of
sorts in the planned community of Woodland, Maryland.
Authoritative, debonair, self-confident, his reputation for
engaging in one casual relationship after another almost
overshadows his prowess as a doctor. In reality, Greg
dates more out of necessity than anything else, since he
has to attend one social function after another. He con-
siders most of the events boring and wishes he could
spend more time with his children. But his profession is a
difficult and demanding one—and being both father and
mother to four kids isn't any less so. A thoughtful, generous, sometimes befuddled father, Greg tries to do it all.
Cerebral, he uses his intellect and skill rather than physical
strength to win his victories. However, he never expected
to come up against one Mary Magdalene May!

Heroine:
MARY MAGDALENE MAY, called Maggie by her friends, is the thirty-two-year-old mother of three children. She has shoulder-length auburn hair, and green eyes that shout her Irish heritage. With high cheekbones and an upturned nose covered with a smattering of freckles, Maggie thinks of herself more as the girl-next-door type. Certainly, she believes, she could never be one of Greg Wilder's beautiful escorts.

Setting: The small town of Woodland, Maryland

The Story:
Surgeon Greg Wilder wanted to court the feisty and beautiful widow who'd been caring for his four kids, but she just wouldn't let him past her doorstep! Sure that his interest was only casual, and that he preferred more sophisticated women, Maggie May vowed to keep Greg at arm's length. But he wouldn't take no for an answer. And once he'd crashed through her defenses and pulled her into his arms, he was tireless—and reckless—in his campaign to win her over. Maggie had found it tough enough to resist one determined doctor; now he threatened to call in his kids and hers as reinforcements—seven rowdy snags to romance!

Cover scene:
As if romancing Maggie weren't hard enough, Greg can't seem to find time to spend with her without their children around. Stealing a private moment on the stairs in Maggie's house, Greg and Maggie embrace. She is standing one step above him, but she still has to look up at him to see into his eyes. Greg's hands are on her hips, and her hands are resting on his shoulders. Maggie is wearing a very sheer, short pink nightgown, and Greg has on wheat-colored jeans and a navy and yellow striped rugby shirt. Do they have time to kiss?

THE HOMETOWN HUNK CONTEST

IN A CLASS BY ITSELF
(Originally Published as LOVESWEPT #66)
By Sandra Brown

COVER NOTES

The Characters:

Hero:
LOGAN WEBSTER would have no trouble posing for a
Scandinavian travel poster. His wheat-colored hair always
seems to be tousled, defying attempts to control it, and
falls across his wide forehead. Thick eyebrows one shade
darker than his hair accentuate his crystal blue eyes. He
has a slender nose that flairs slightly over a mouth that
testifies to both sensitivity and strength. The faint lines
around his eyes and alongside his mouth give the impression that reaching the ripe age of 30 wasn't all fun and
games for him. Logan's square, determined jaw is punctuated by a vertical cleft. His broad shoulders and narrow
waist add to his tall, lean appearance.

Personality traits:
Logan Webster has had to scrape and save and fight for
everything he's gotten. Born into a poor farm family, he
was driven to succeed and overcome his "wrong side of
the tracks" image. His businesses include cattle, real estate, and natural gas. Now a pillar of the community,
Logan's life has been a true rags-to-riches story. Only
Sandra Brown's own words can describe why he is masculinity epitomized: "Logan had 'the walk,' that saddle-
tramp saunter that was inherent to native Texan men,
passed down through generations of cowboys. It was, without even trying to be, sexy. The unconscious roll of the
hips, the slow strut, the flexed knees, the slouching stance,
the deceptive laziness that hid a latent aggressiveness."
Wow! And not only does he have "the walk," but he's fun

and generous and kind. Even with his wealth, he feels at home living in his small hometown with simple, hard-working, middle-class, backbone-of-America folks. A born leader, people automatically gravitate toward him.

Heroine:
DANI QUINN is a sophisticated twenty-eight-year-old woman. Dainty, her body compact, she is utterly feminine. Dani's pale, lustrous hair is moonlight and honey spun together, and because it is very straight, she usually wears it in a chignon. With golden eyes to match her golden hair, Dani is the one woman Logan hasn't been able to get off his mind for the ten years they've been apart.

Setting: Primarily on Logan's ranch in East Texas.

The Story:
Ten years had passed since Dani Quinn had graduated from high school in the small Texas town, ten years since the night her elopement with Logan Webster had ended in disaster. Now Dani approached her tenth reunion with uncertainty. Logan would be there . . . Logan, the only man who'd ever made her shiver with desire and need, but would she have the courage to face the fury in his eyes? She couldn't defend herself against his anger and hurt—to do so would demand she reveal the secret sorrow she shared with no one. Logan's touch had made her his so long ago. Could he reach past the pain to make her his for all time?

Cover Scene:
It's sunset, and Logan and Dani are standing beside the swimming pool on his ranch, embracing. The pool is surrounded by semitropical plants and lush flower beds. In the distance, acres of rolling pasture land resembling a green lake undulate into dense, piney woods. Dani is wearing a strapless, peacock blue bikini and sandals with leather ties that wrap around her ankles. Her hair is straight and loose, falling to the middle of her back. Logan has on a light-colored pair of corduroy shorts and a short-sleeved designer knit shirt in a pale shade of yellow.

THE HOMETOWN HUNK CONTEST

C.J.'S FATE

(Originally Published as LOVESWEPT #32)

By Kay Hooper

COVER NOTES

The Characters:

Hero:

FATE WESTON easily could have walked straight off an Indian reservation. His raven black hair and strong, well-molded features testify to his heritage. But somewhere along the line genetics threw Fate a curve—his eyes are the deepest, darkest blue imaginable! Above those blue eyes are dark slanted eyebrows, and fanning out from those eyes are faint laugh lines—the only sign of the fact that he's thirty-four years old. Tall, Fate moves with easy, loose-limbed grace. Although he isn't an athlete, Fate takes very good care of himself, and it shows in his strong physique. Striking at first glance and fascinating with each succeeding glance, the serious expressions on his face make him look older than his years, but with one smile he looks boyish again.

Personality traits:

Fate possesses a keen sense of humor. His heavy-lidded, intelligent eyes are capable of concealment, but there is a shrewdness in them that reveals the man hadn't needed college or a law degree to be considered intelligent. The set of his head tells you that he is proud—perhaps even a bit arrogant. He is attractive and perfectly well aware of that fact. Unconventional, paradoxical, tender, silly, lusty, gentle, comical, serious, absurd, and endearing are all words that come to mind when you think of Fate. He is not ashamed to be everything a man can be. A defense attorney by profession, one can detect a bit of frustrated actor in his character. More than anything else, though, it's the impression of humor about him—reinforced by the elusive dimple in his cheek—that makes Fate Weston a scrumptious hero!

Heroine:
C.J. ADAMS is a twenty-six-year-old research librarian. Unaware of her own attractiveness, C.J. tends to play down her pixylike figure and tawny gold eyes. But once she meets Fate, she no longer feels that her short, burnished copper curls and the sprinkling of freckles on her nose make her unappealing. He brings out the vixen in her, and changes the smart, bookish woman who professed to have no interest in men into the beautiful, sexy woman she really was all along. Now, if only he could get her to tell him what C.J. stands for!

Setting: Ski lodge in Aspen, Colorado

The Story:
C.J. Adams had been teased enough about her seeming lack of interest in the opposite sex. On a ski trip with her five best friends, she impulsively embraced a handsome stranger, pretending they were secret lovers—and the delighted lawyer who joined in her impetuous charade seized the moment to deepen the kiss. Astonished at his reaction, C.J. tried to nip their romance in the bud—but found herself nipping at his neck instead! She had met her match in a man who could answer her witty remarks with clever ripostes of his own, and a lover whose caresses aroused in her a passionate need she'd never suspected that she could feel. Had destiny somehow tossed them together?

Cover Scene:
C.J. and Fate virtually have the ski slopes to themselves early one morning, and they take advantage of it! Frolicking in a snow drift, Fate is covering C.J. with snow—and kisses! They are flushed from the cold weather and from the excitement of being in love. C.J. is wearing a sky-blue, one-piece, tight-fitting ski outfit that zips down the front. Fate is wearing a navy blue parka and matching ski pants.

THE HOMETOWN HUNK CONTEST

THE LADY AND THE UNICORN
(Originally Published as LOVESWEPT #29)
By Iris Johansen

COVER NOTES

The Characters:

Hero:
Not classically handsome, RAFE SANTINE's blunt, craggy
features reinforce the quality of overpowering virility about
him. He has wide, Slavic cheekbones and a bold, thrusting chin, which give the impression of strength and authority. Thick black eyebrows are set over piercing dark
eyes. He wears his heavy, dark hair long. His large frame
measures in at almost six feet four inches, and it's hard to
believe that a man with such brawny shoulders and strong
thighs could exhibit the pantherlike grace which charac-
terizes Rafe's movements. Rafe Santine is definitely a man
to be reckoned with, and heroine Janna Cannon does just
that!

Personality traits:
Our hero is a man who radiates an aura of power and
danger, and women find him intriguing and irresistible.
Rafe Santine is a self-made billionaire at the age of thirty-
eight. Almost entirely self-educated, he left school at six-
teen to work on his first construction job, and by the time
he was twenty-three, he owned the company. From there
he branched out into real estate, computers, and oil. Rafe
reportedly changes mistresses as often as he changes shirts.
His reputation for ruthless brilliance has been earned over
years of fighting to the top of the economic ladder from
the slums of New York. His gruff manner and hard personality hide the tender, vulnerable side of him. Rafe also
possesses an insatiable thirst for knowledge that is a
passion with him. Oddly enough, he has a wry sense of

humor that surfaces unexpectedly from time to time. And, though cynical to the extreme, he never lets his natural skepticism interfere with his innate sense of justice.

Heroine:
JANNA CANNON, a game warden for a small wildlife preserve, is a very dedicated lady. She is tall at five feet nine inches and carries herself in a stately way. Her long hair is dark brown and is usually twisted into a single thick braid in back. Of course, Rafe never lets her keep her hair braided when they make love! Janna is one quarter Cherokee Indian by heritage, and she possesses the dark eyes and skin of her ancestors.

Setting: Rafe's estate in Carmel, California

The Story:
Janna Cannon scaled the high walls of Rafe Santine's private estate, afraid of nothing and determined to appeal to the powerful man who could save her beloved animal preserve. She bewitched his guard dogs, then cast a spell of enchantment over him as well. Janna's profound grace, her caring nature, made the tough and proud Rafe grow mercurial in her presence. She offered him a gift he'd never risked reaching out for before—but could he trust his own emotions enough to open himself to her love?

Cover Scene:
In the gazebo overlooking the rugged cliffs at the edge of the Pacific Ocean, Rafe and Janna share a passionate moment together. The gazebo is made of redwood and the interior is small and cozy. Scarlet cushions cover the benches, and matching scarlet curtains hang from the eaves, caught back by tasseled sashes to permit the sea breeze to whip through the enclosure. Rafe is wearing black suede pants and a charcoal gray crew-neck sweater. Janna is wearing a safari-style khaki shirt-and-slacks outfit and suede desert boots. They embrace against the breathtaking backdrop of wild, crashing, white-crested waves pounding the rocks and cliffs below.

THE HOMETOWN HUNK CONTEST

CHARADE
(Originally Published as LOVESWEPT #74)
By Joan Elliott Pickart

COVER NOTES

The Characters:

Hero:
The phrase tall, dark, and handsome was coined to describe TENNES WHITNEY. His coal black hair reaches past his collar in back, and his fathomless steel gray eyes are framed by the kind of thick, dark lashes that a woman would kill to have. Darkly tanned, Tennes has a straight nose and a square chin, with—you guessed it!—a Kirk Douglas cleft. Tennes oozes masculinity and virility. He's a handsome son-of-a-gun!

Personality traits:
A shrewd, ruthless business tycoon, Tennes is a man of strength and principle. He's perfected the art of buying floundering companies and turning them around financially, then selling them at a profit. He possesses a sixth sense about business—in short, he's a winner! But there are two sides to his personality. Always in cool command, Tennes, who fears no man or challenge, is rendered emotionally vulnerable when faced with his elderly aunt's illness. His deep devotion to the woman who raised him clearly casts him as a warm, compassionate guy—not at all like the tough-as-nails executive image he presents. Leave it to heroine Whitney Jordan to discover the real man behind the complicated enigma.

Heroine:
WHITNEY JORDAN's russet-colored hair floats past her shoulders in glorious waves. Her emerald green eyes, full breasts, and long, slender legs—not to mention her peaches-

and-cream complexion—make her eye-poppingly attractive. How can Tennes resist the twenty-six-year-old beauty? And how can Whitney consider becoming serious with him? If their romance flourishes, she may end up being Whitney Whitney!

Setting: Los Angeles, California

The Story:
One moment writer Whitney Jordan was strolling the aisles of McNeil's Department Store, plotting the untimely demise of a soap opera heartthrob; the next, she was nearly knocked over by a real-life stunner who implored her to be his fiancée! The ailing little gray-haired aunt who'd raised him had one final wish, he said—to see her dear nephew Tennes married to the wonderful girl he'd described in his letters . . . only that girl hadn't existed—until now! Tennes promised the masquerade would last only through lunch, but Whitney gave such an inspired performance that Aunt Olive refused to let her go. And what began as a playful romantic deception grew more breathlessly real by the minute. . . .

Cover Scene:
Whitney's living room is bright and cheerful. The gray carpeting and blue sofa with green and blue throw pillows gives the apartment a cool but welcoming appearance. Sitting on the sofa next to Tennes, Whitney is wearing a black crepe dress that is simply cut but stunning. It is cut low over her breasts and held at the shoulders by thin straps. The skirt falls to her knees in soft folds and the bodice is nipped in at the waist with a matching belt. She has on black high heels, but prefers not to wear any jewelry to spoil the simplicity of the dress. Tennes is dressed in a black suit with a white silk shirt and a deep red tie.

THE HOMETOWN HUNK CONTEST

FOR THE LOVE OF SAMI
(Originally Published as LOVESWEPT #34)
By Fayrene Preston

COVER NOTES

Hero:
DANIEL PARKER-ST. JAMES is every woman's dream come
true. With glossy black hair and warm, reassuring blue
eyes, he makes our heroine melt with just a glance. Daniel's lean face is chiseled into assertive planes. His lips are
full and firmly sculptured, and his chin has the determined and arrogant thrust to it only a man who's sure of
himself can carry off. Daniel has a lot in common with
Clark Kent. Both wear glasses, and when Daniel removes
them to make love to Sami, she thinks he really is
Superman!

Personality traits:
Daniel Parker-St. James is one of the Twin Cities' most
respected attorneys. He's always in the news, either in the
society columns with his latest society lady, or on the
front page with his headline cases. He's brilliant and takes
on only the toughest cases—usually those that involve
millions of dollars. Daniel has a reputation for being a
deadly opponent in the courtroom. Because he's from a
socially prominent family and is a Harvard graduate, it's
expected that he'll run for the Senate one day. Distinguished-
looking and always distinctively dressed—he's fastidious
about his appearance—Daniel gives off an unassailable air
of authority and absolute control.

Heroine:
SAMUELINA (SAMI) ADKINSON is secretly a wealthy heiress. No one would guess. She lives in a converted ware-
house loft, dresses to suit no one but herself, and dabbles
in the creative arts. Sami is twenty-six years old, with

long, honey-colored hair. She wears soft, wispy bangs and has very thick brown lashes framing her golden eyes. Of medium height, Sami has to look up to gaze into Daniel's deep blue eyes.

Setting: St. Paul, Minnesota

The Story:
Unpredictable heiress Sami Adkinson had endeared herself to the most surprising people—from the bag ladies in the park she protected . . . to the mobster who appointed himself her guardian . . . to her exasperated but loving friends. Then Sami was arrested while demonstrating to save baby seals, and it took powerful attorney Daniel Parker-St. James to bail her out. Daniel was smitten, soon cherishing Sami and protecting her from her night fears. Sami reveled in his love—and resisted it too. And holding on to Sami, Daniel discovered, was like trying to hug quicksilver. . . .

Cover Scene:
The interior of Daniel's house is very grand and supremely formal, the decor sophisticated, refined, and quietly tasteful, just like Daniel himself. Rich traditional fabrics cover plush oversized custom sofas and Regency wing chairs. Queen Anne furniture is mixed with Chippendale and is subtly complemented with Oriental accent pieces. In the library, floor-to-ceiling bookcases filled with rare books provide the backdrop for Sami and Daniel's embrace. Sami is wearing a gold satin sheath gown. The dress has a high neckline, but in back is cut provocatively to the waist. Her jewels are exquisite. The necklace is made up of clusters of flowers created by large, flawless diamonds. From every cluster a huge, perfectly matched teardrop emerald hangs. The earrings are composed of an even larger flower cluster, and an equally huge teardrop-shaped emerald hangs from each one. Daniel is wearing a classic, elegant tuxedo.

LOVESWEPT® HOMETOWN HUNK CONTEST

OFFICIAL RULES

> IN A CLASS BY ITSELF by Sandra Brown
> FOR THE LOVE OF SAMI by Fayrene Preston
> C.J.'S FATE by Kay Hooper
> THE LADY AND THE UNICORN by Iris Johansen
> CHARADE by Joan Elliott Pickart
> DARLING OBSTACLES by Barbara Boswell

1. NO PURCHASE NECESSARY. Enter the HOMETOWN HUNK contest by completing the Official Entry Form below and enclosing a sharp color full-length photograph (easy to see details, with the photo being no smaller than 2½″ × 3½″) of the man you think perfectly represents one of the heroes from the above-listed books which are described in the accompanying Loveswept cover notes. Please be sure to fill out the Official Entry Form completely, and also be sure to clearly print on the back of the man's photograph the man's name, address, city, state, zip code, telephone number, date of birth, your name, address, city, state, zip code, telephone number, your relationship, if any, to the man (e.g. wife, girlfriend) as well as the title of the Loveswept book for which you are entering the man. If you do not have an Official Entry Form, you can print all of the required information on a 3″ × 5″ card and attach it to the photograph with all the necessary information printed on the back of the photograph as well. YOUR HERO MUST SIGN BOTH THE BACK OF THE OFFICIAL ENTRY FORM (OR 3″ × 5″ CARD) AND THE PHOTOGRAPH TO SIGNIFY HIS CONSENT TO BEING ENTERED IN THE CONTEST. Completed entries should be sent to:

> BANTAM BOOKS
> HOMETOWN HUNK CONTEST
> Department CN
> 666 Fifth Avenue
> New York, New York 10102–0023

All photographs and entries become the property of Bantam Books and will not be returned under any circumstances.

2. Six men will be chosen by the Loveswept authors as a HOMETOWN HUNK (one HUNK per Loveswept title). By entering the contest, each winner and each person who enters a winner agrees to abide by Bantam Books' rules and to be subject to Bantam Books' eligibility requirements. Each winning HUNK and each person who enters a winner will be required to sign all papers deemed necessary by Bantam Books before receiving any prize. Each winning HUNK will be flown via **United Airlines** from his closest United Airlines-serviced city to New York City and will stay at the ⊿⊿ S∪N∖⊓ Hotel—the ideal hotel for business or pleasure in midtown Manhattan—for two nights. Winning HUNKS' meals and hotel transfers will be provided by Bantam Books. Travel and hotel arrangements are made by *RELIABLE TRAVEL INTERNATIONAL, INC.* and are subject to availability and to Bantam Books' date requirements. Each winning HUNK will pose with a female model at a photographer's studio for a photograph that will serve as the basis of a Loveswept front cover. Each winning HUNK will receive a $150.00 modeling fee. Each winning HUNK will be required to sign an Affidavit of Eligibility and Model's Release supplied by Bantam Books. (Approximate retail value of HOMETOWN HUNK'S PRIZE: $900.00). The six people who send in a winning HOMETOWN HUNK photograph that is used by Bantam will receive free for one year each, LOVESWEPT romance paperback books published by Bantam during that year. (Approximate retail value: $180.00.) Each person who submits a winning photograph

will also be required to sign an Affidavit of Eligibility and Promotional Release supplied by Bantam Books. All winning HUNKS' (as well as the people who submit the winning photographs) names, addresses, biographical data and likenesses may be used by Bantam Books for publicity and promotional purposes without any additional compensation. There will be no prize substitutions or cash equivalents made.

3. All completed entries must be received by Bantam Books no later than September 15, 1988. Bantam Books is not responsible for lost or misdirected entries. The finalists will be selected by Loveswept editors and the six winning HOMETOWN HUNKS will be selected by the six authors of the participating Loveswept books. Winners will be selected on the basis of how closely the judges believe they reflect the descriptions of the books' heroes. Winners will be notified on or about October 31, 1988. If there are insufficient entries or if in the judges' opinions, no entry is suitable or adequately reflects the descriptions of the hero(s) in the book(s), Bantam may decide not to award a prize for the applicable book(s) and may reissue the book(s) at its discretion.

4. The contest is open to residents of the U.S. and Canada, except the Province of Quebec, and is void where prohibited by law. All federal and local regulations apply. Employees of Reliable Travel International, Inc., United Airlines, the Summit Hotel, and the Bantam Doubleday Dell Publishing Group, Inc., their subsidiaries and affiliates, and their immediate families are ineligible to enter.

5. For an extra copy of the Official Rules, the Official Entry Form, and the accompanying Loveswept cover notes, send your request and a self-addressed stamped envelope (Vermont and Washington State residents need not affix postage) before August 20, 1988 to the address listed in Paragraph 1 above.

LOVESWEPT* HOMETOWN HUNK OFFICIAL ENTRY FORM

BANTAM BOOKS
HOMETOWN HUNK CONTEST
Dept. CN
666 Fifth Avenue
New York, New York 10102–0023

HOMETOWN HUNK CONTEST

YOUR NAME_____

YOUR ADDRESS_____

CITY_____ STATE_____ ZIP_____

THE NAME OF THE LOVESWEPT BOOK FOR WHICH YOU ARE ENTERING THIS PHOTO

_____by_____

YOUR RELATIONSHIP TO YOUR HERO_____

YOUR HERO'S NAME_____

YOUR HERO'S ADDRESS_____

CITY_____ STATE_____ ZIP_____.

YOUR HERO'S TELEPHONE #_____

YOUR HERO'S DATE OF BIRTH_____

YOUR HERO'S SIGNATURE CONSENTING TO HIS PHOTOGRAPH ENTRY

_____